SAVING TAYLA

AMANDA KAITLYN

BOOKS BY AMANDA KAITLYN

The Beautifully Broken Series

Finding Beautiful

Breaking Lucas

This Beautiful Love

Dare To Love

Saving Tayla

Unwrapping Lucas (Coming 2020)

Remembering Ben (TBD)

Standalones

Breathe With Me

One Night With Lyric (TBD)

Black Harts Motorcycle Club

Until Us

The Broken In Us (TBD)

The Salvation Of Us (TBD)

For Brittany
I know the darkness can seem insurmountable,
but I promise, one day you'll find the light at the end
of it.

For anyone that has ever suffered from addiction,
whatever it may be. Know that you aren't alone.
For help or guidance, call the hot-line at American
Addiction Centers:
1-877-883-0988

FOREWORD

If you have read my books, you know what you'll find beneath the covers of each one. Love. Loss. Pain. Forgiveness. Asher and Tayla's story was no different. But their story was very personal for me, and I want you to know why.

As I grew up, I witnessed addiction take hold of one of the most important people in my life and from the experience of it, I can tell you, it wasn't easy. It was a living, breathing demon inside of her that, no matter her strength, bravery, even her good nature and kind heart, she couldn't control or overcome.

The only way to survive it is to seek help. From family. From friends. From those who love you and only want the best for you.

In this story, Tayla has the same road to recovery my sister had. I won't sugarcoat it and I won't shy away from it. So, this, *this* is Tayla's story.

It's raw. Gritty. Real. Difficult. Beautiful.

Have your tissues ready, because this will not only make you cry but will also make you *feel*. And that's all I've ever wanted to do with my words.

Love,

Amanda

~

Addict. I never thought I would use that word to describe myself. I was broken, damaged goods. My ex ruined me, wholly and completely. Because of him, I became addicted to the taste of a high I quickly felt I couldn't live without. My once bright world was so dark, I couldn't see my way out of it.

I *was lost.*

A year later, I was free of that damaged man and ready to start living, again.

Fighting every day to be sober and become the woman I used to be was my top priority, now.

Asher tore into my life like a *hurricane*, wrecking my perfectly laid plans in his path. I didn't have time to fall for a man like him. He had a dirty mouth that melted me but he was dangerous, I knew that. My heart wanted to give into him, but my mind knew better.

Loving him was my downfall.

"*O*ne last push, Tayla. You can do this."

No. No, I couldn't.

Looking down at the doctor as she sat between my legs, my head shook vehemently.

I couldn't do this. The physical pain I could bear, but the knowledge of the loss that was waiting for me once my baby was born?

I didn't know how I'd survive it. But I would.

For him. My little Spencer. Named after my granddad, his name was the one condition I'd given the couple that would be raising my boy once I signed the papers, *signed him over to them.*

It would be that easy. One scribble on the dotted line of a paper I probably wouldn't even read and I wouldn't be his mom, anymore.

I knew I wasn't ready to be a mom. Not when the only reason I was sober was because of my pregnancy. Not when I was unable to take care of myself, day by day never-mind a whole other human that would rely on me for... *everything*. I didn't even have a job. Or a place to rest my head at night that wasn't a half-way house or a shelter. I was a broken mess and anyone that saw me could see that.

I didn't want a life like that for him. I wanted him to be happy, whole, even. I wanted him to play little league and get an A in Math. I wanted him to ride his bike around a nice neighborhood and do all of the things normal kids did.

And as much as I hated to admit it, I couldn't give that to him.

I was on the verge of hot, stinging tears before I felt familiar hands clasp my shoulders, rubbing them gently as if to say *it's okay*. I looked up to see Scarlet standing at the head of my hospital bed, her eyes filled with encouragement and love I didn't deserve but needed more than anything right then. My sister was here. I'd put her through so much, let her down countless times, yet here she was when anyone else would have written me off.

"Okay. I'm ready." Just one more push. I could do this. I had to.

Gathering strength from deep, deep inside of me, I gripped the metal bars on either side of the bed tightly, my bare feet held by the doctor's insistent hands as I *pushed*.

Something pivotal inside of me shifted as my baby boy came into the world, his loud, beautiful cries the best sound I was sure I'd ever heard. All of my fears for this day evaporated in the wake of the miracle that was my son.

"Oh my God, Tay. He's..." Scarlet's hand grabbed onto mine in a tight squeeze as the nurse took my baby boy away, placing him on a table nearby to check him. My eyes couldn't help following him, as fear that something was wrong coursed through me.

"What? Scar, is he okay?" *He has to be okay.*

"They're just checking him." Her words didn't soothe me, like I thought they would. Panic was welling up inside of me, the idea of him being any- thing less than perfect an unbearable one.

When my baby was wrapped in a blue blanket and lowered to my chest, everything inside of me calmed, melted at the sight of this beautiful, innocent thing made from a life filled with sadness and pain and mistakes I wished to God I could rewrite.

His little fingers wrapped around my thumb, squeezing in that way babies do and right in that mo- ment, I knew I wanted to keep him. I wanted him to be mine, but knew that if I kept him, it would be self- ish. It wouldn't ensure his happiness, his safety. And that was *all* that mattered to me.

Gliding my thumb gently, reverently over his cheek, I wished things could be different. So much different. If only I'd made better choices, if only I had the faith that I could be a good mother to this precious boy...

It was just like a dream. Holding him and seeing him, yet knowing that everything I was feeling was fleeting. No matter how much I wished for it, wanted it, this moment wasn't mine.

How could I let him go? How could I go back to my life as I once knew it, when I could be a mom to such a perfect boy? As the questions and doubts flitted through my mind, I looked back down at him, knowing I had limited time to memorize him, *touch* him.

His face was upturned as he rested on my chest but his eyes were still tightly closed, as if he knew just how hard it would be if I had to look into his eyes as I

3

said goodbye. I wasn't sure if he would have the hazel eyes that ran in my family, but I couldn't help hoping he would. My fingers traced his, counting to ten just to be sure. I repeated this until I was sure I had my baby boy memorized from head to toe. Only then, did I turn my face away, knowing this was goodbye, the only one I'd ever get with him. It took everything inside of me to close my eyes against the sight of his angelic face.

I couldn't bear to look at him when I knew I was about to lose him, forever.

In a few, short, hours he would belong to another family.

"Take him, please." My voice was a plea, an apology to the little boy I'd never know, never get to see grow up.

"Tayla, you have time –" I felt my sisters' hand on my face, trying, and failing to sway me from the choice that was made well before today.

As much as I wished I could keep him, I knew it was time to let him go. *Even if it broke me in the process.*

"Please, Scar." My eyes burned with the tears that I knew were coming and once they started, I wasn't sure if they would stop.

"I have to let him go." Silence settled after the words slipped from my lips and the deafening sound of that silence lasted until the weight of him was lifted from my chest. Then, the only sound in the room were the crushing sobs that his loss caused.

1

TAYLA

ONE YEAR LATER

"*D*on't go, Scar." I squeezed her hand in mine, my chest tight with the anguished pain I saw shining in her eyes. Pain I knew I was the reason for.

I'd done this to her. My own sister.

How many times had we been here? How many times had I plead with her for a chance, yet another *godforsaken* chance to make everything right between us, again? And how many nights did she spend searching for me, looking down every dark alley in hopes of finding me before it was too late?

Too many to count.

I was a lost cause. I would *always* go back to the high that I craved, using any drug I could to chase away the pain my reality had become. This time, though, I hoped – no, I *prayed* – that I would make it. I hoped that this was the one that stuck.

"I don't want to leave you, Tay. But seeing you like this hurts me, too."

"Don't." Squeezing her slim, pale fingers in mine even more tightly, I begged her, in hopes that she could see the desperation for forgiveness that filled my mind and tortured my soul.

I needed her. I needed her to *believe* I could do this. I could get clean, once and for all. Because if she didn't believe I could, how could I?

"Please," I whispered into her hair, as something that felt a whole lot like hope shadowed through my veins.

"Okay, Tay. *Okay*." My body sagged against hers the instant I heard those words and I thanked God for them.

One last chance, I told myself. Closing my eyes, I swore to myself that I wouldn't disappoint her, this time.

This time would be different.

I just hoped that vow wasn't yet another broken promise I made to myself.

2

TAYLA

"*W*hat are you afraid of, Tayla?"

My eyes snapped up from my lap as I heard my name, finding kind eyes centered on me and silent acceptance lingering in the air. But that same silence made me nervous. I didn't want to have to talk about why I was here.

I didn't even want to be here, in the first place. I didn't belong in a place like this. *Didn't I?*

When had it all gone wrong? I asked myself that question more than I'd like to admit. The answer was an easy one.

Trent. The man I'd thought was the love of my life, *the one*. But he turned into another man all together. Cocky. Mean. Manipulative. When we met, I didn't know him as that man. I knew an entirely different guy. He was kind and generous and loving to me, right from the start.

We're meant to be, Tay. You and me. I believed those lies he told me in the beginning. I thought his jealousy was endearing, a sign that he loved and wanted only me. Soon, I was living under his roof, allowing him to pull me deeper and deeper into his world and disappearing from mine completely.

He was the one that gave me my first taste of the high. He was the one that set this all-in motion. But that was a cop-out, wasn't it?

Because when he asked me if I wanted a hit, I never said no. I was weak. *Stupid*. I didn't even know who I was, anymore.

Junkie. User. Liar. Thief. Those were the words I'd come to associate with. I couldn't blame anyone, but myself.

"Tayla?"

"Huh?" Raising my head, I looked Dr. Sloan in the eyes and saw the pity in her depths, the sadness for me.

"What are you afraid of, Tayla?" Her words were spoken with care, no malice or incrimination in her voice. But being vulnerable if front of near strangers wasn't something I was used to. The looks of pity and silent judgement were ones I couldn't handle. Because I knew they were right to write me off. I didn't even recognize myself, these days.

"I'm not afraid." *Lie.*

Her blonde head tilted slightly to the side as those always understanding eyes narrowed on me. She didn't believe me for even a second.

"Everybody has fears in life. Everybody. It doesn't matter if you're three years old or thirty. It's finding what those fears are and what causes them that can allow you to overcome them. Or else you'll always be weighed down by those fears. Can you share yours with the group? It's okay if you don't want to."

Where did I even start? It wasn't a tangible thing

8

that I was fearful of. There wasn't a monster under my bed that I could will away.

It wasn't a lion, tiger, or bear. No, my biggest fear ran so much deeper inside of me. It stopped me from living, because I didn't think I deserved a happy life when I'd hurt so many people around me, for so long. It kept me from forgiving myself for the pain I had caused, the sadness and the grief that those around me were left with and it was all caused by *me*.

Me, me, me. I was the one that caused my father's heart to break... my sister to lose her dream job because she had to stay with me in the hospital, one too many times... my friends to distance themselves from me, because all I could see was my darkness.

It was why I needed the escape. Why, at the first chance I could get, I would find my fix. I just wanted to be *free*.

Free from the sense of loss I felt every time I opened my eyes and felt the emptiness inside of me. Free from the sorrow that affected every facet of my life. Maybe she was right. Maybe I needed to face that fear, before I could get past it. It was painfully obvious to me, in that moment, that I wasn't getting past my grief. All I was doing was hiding from it.

I exhaled a shaky breath and nodded in acceptance, finding the soft look in her eyes comforting against the dark place my mind had become.

My throat felt dry and cracked, my heart heavy with the weight of the truth I would tell these strangers, these people who felt the pain of regret and past mistakes, just as I had.

It was my truth to tell. My mistakes to bear. My amends to make. And I was *terrified* to face it. Face all the hurt I'd caused. But I had to. I *had* to.

"One year ago, I decided to give my little boy up for adoption. I thought it was the right thing to do... no, *no*, it *was* the right thing. Maybe not for me, but for him? It was the best thing. I wanted what was best for him, but I never understood what it would mean to not have him with me. Not to feel him move in my stomach or kick me in the middle of the night. It hurt... so much. Giving birth and then handing him over to the social worker so that he could be placed with his new family was the hardest thing I'd ever had to do. I never dealt with that pain until I came here. I don't know how to do this."

My chest was so tight with the loss of him that I had to stop, to take a breath, to let myself, if only for a moment, feel the gravity of the words I knew I had to admit in order to move past it all.

I didn't regret my pregnancy or his birth for a moment. I loved him more than I could put into words. I didn't think a love like that could go away, even if it could— I didn't want it to.

I was his mom and he would never know me. Never know how much I missed him and wished things could have been different. Trent hadn't stuck around long enough for me to tell him my plan of giving our baby up for adoption, in the hopes that he would grow up never knowing the kind of dark, dismal place I was in when he was conceived. Even if Trent wanted the baby I was carrying, I wasn't anywhere near ready to be a mother.

I was barely able to care for myself, as it was.

My baby boy wouldn't have a fighting chance if he'd stayed with me, I knew that. So, I gave him up. I let him go. And then I took another hit, knowing the loss of him would never fade, even if I took every drug

I could find. That kind of pain would linger. And it had.

"I guess what I'm trying to say is that my biggest fear is never seeing him again."

Countless hushed whispers met my ears as the circle of fellow broken souls took in my truth. I waited for the judgment, the harsh words of criticism and blame. I closed my eyes and waited for those hurtful words to be slung my way, without thought of the guilt and remorse I lived with, every day.

But those words didn't come. The room didn't explode into chaos. Instead, I heard the condolences I knew I wasn't worthy of. Whispered sorry's and softly spoken prayers filled the room. I felt my heart sag underneath the weight of my regret, my sorrow and it was only then that I allowed myself to feel that sadness, that ripping, burning pain I tried so hard to destroy with my addiction and my many, many mistakes.

"Shh, let it all out now, Tayla. You're *safe* here. You're going to be alright."

My throat stung with a sob I'd been holding in for far too long as warm, sheltering arms wrapped around me in the most comforting embrace a near-stranger could give.

"T—thank you," I mumbled through my tears, something that felt a whole lot like hope finally peeking through the layers of darkness that had consumed me for so long.

"It's okay, now." Her whisper was a simple one, yet somehow, I finally believed it.

11

3

ASHER

"*J*ust start when you're ready. I'll have to hear you raw before we record anything."

"Gotcha. You want me to play? Or just sing?" Blake Reynolds, my newest artist stood behind the glass in front of me, his guitar strapped around his neck, fingers idling on the strings as he waited for instruction.

Adjusting the pitch just a bit on my end, I peered through the glass of the sound box and shook my head. I wanted to hear him raw, without anything diminishing the voice on him. I'd heard him for the first-time last week, at a packed bar in Dallas and knew he had something special.

"Naw. Let's start this simple, alright?"

With a nod, he moved behind the mic and readied to start his song. The glint in his eyes told me music wasn't just something he did for fun. It was his *passion*. What made him tick. That's what would set him apart from all the other country artists struggling to break through right now.

As he began singing a slower version of the original, he'd sung on his demo, I sat back and closed my eyes for a few moments, allowing myself to just *listen*.

He was good. His voice may have been young, new and uncut but shit, it was good. Soft, yet deep. Gritted with enough emotion to bring depth to a song that was anything, but. And it had a southern twang to it that was just prominent enough to be alluring, yet not overpowering.

Opening my eyes, I watched his demeanor from the control room. It was as if he were on stage again.

And he was blowing it out of the damn park.

Though he was forced to remain behind the large microphone that was centered behind the glass of the sound box, everything about his performance was dominating, real and raw. His eyes held the torture betrayed by the song he sung and I noticed the way his fingers wrapped tightly around the microphone, as if everything in his life had led him to this very song and he sung it as if his life depended on it. I'd seen more than a few artists clutch it like that, but those performances had been choppy, at best. Blake's desperation stemmed from emotion and feeling for the music he sung, not because of nervousness or unease. His voice took on a breathier tone as he finished his song and the music came to an end, yet the emotion the melody held didn't end, because I could still see it clearly across his face.

"That was great, Blake. Do you want to have a listen?"

A large, relieved grin spread over the kid's face as he nodded once and I gave him a firm slap on the shoulder as he passed me.

Standing in the doorway, I watched him take a seat behind the control desk and hit 'play' in order to replay the track. His face gave nothing away for a few minutes and I stood back, wondering what he was hearing from his voice; knowing it could take a while for him to truly believe its authenticity, its *talent*. When his face spread with another one of his infectious smiles, I knew he was feeling it. His deep laugh echoed through the room and I grinned, because having a happy artist was especially important to me when working with someone, even more so that it was Blake.

We'd become almost friends over the past few days and, given the darkness I knew his personal life was at present, I felt a need to bring some joy to his life. If the light in his eyes or the disbelieving shake of his head was any indication, I had succeeded in fuckin' strides.

"You look happy."

"Shit, I didn't think I had it in me, man. I thought I was good, but this? I didn't expect this."

Then I was the one who was shaking my head in disbelief.

"I'm not gonna lie and pretend that this industry isn't hard to make a name in, because it damn sure is. But I think that, with the right sound and the right push, you've got a hell of a good shot, Blake."

He stood quickly, trying, I was sure, to blink back the sudden emotion in his eyes as he reached out a steady hand to me and I took it, shaking hands with the man I was sure was going to the top of the country music game soon. But telling him that was like a promise, and I couldn't give that to him. So many things went into producing and backing an artist and one decision, one split second mistake, could cost him everything.

14

But I had a feeling he was worth the risk.

~

"What took you so long?"

"It's nice to see you, too, Charlie."

My sister-in-law stood in the doorway, arms crossed and that signature pissed-off look painted across her face, telling me she wasn't happy with me.

It was my baby sister, Aly's birthday today and as a surprise, Charlie had invited the whole family down from Chicago, where we'd all grown up. My brothers and I lived here now, but my parents still lived in the house we were raised in. My father had remarried a few years back and though I hadn't grown up with Elsa as my mom, she was a mother to me in every sense of the word. She'd never tried to replace the one I'd lost, just filled her shoes in any way she could. It didn't hurt that she was a damn fine cook, too.

They visited on holidays and birthdays and whenever they could take the trip down here. Though, I was pretty sure they spent more of their time here now that they had a grand-baby to spoil.

The smell of something cooking hit my nose and I couldn't help but groan in response, my stomach echoing the sentiment. That makes the annoyance fall away from Charlie's face, her soft smile one of amusement.

Pulling her gently into my side, I squeezed her tight, knowing she couldn't stay annoyed with me for too long. We were family.

"I couldn't help it, Charlie. I was stuck at the studio." I ruffled her hair as I muttered the apology, knowing it would annoy her even more.

An aggravated sigh left her as she peered up at me, trying and failing to keep a stern look on her face. With a dramatic huff, she leaned up to give me a kiss on the cheek before turning to lead the way into the house where I could see everyone was already gathered.

"Ally has Spence playing in the back. You should go say hi. He's been looking forward to seeing y'all all day." Grinning down at her, I nodded, ready to squeeze my nephew after the day I'd had.

When we'd started the studio, I thought I'd spend more time with artists than in an office. Working with Blake today reminded me why we started in the first place and it wasn't to spend the whole day doing paperwork. It was a much needed reminder, that was for damn sure.

I followed Charlie into the kitchen, where the rest of the women of our family seem to have settled. A loud squeal from one in particular permeates the room and I grinned, rocking back on my heels in full knowledge that I've surprised her.

My baby sister comes rushing around the long, granite island in a rush of blonde hair and high-pitched excitement, her arms instantly wrapping around my waist. I quickly lifted her off her feet, spinning her around, as I always did. She'd complain that I made her dizzy later, but I knew she loved the exchange, even if she doesn't admit it. As I squeezed her tight to my chest, I had to bend my knees in order to lower my head to hers, whispering in her ear so only she can hear me.

"Happy birthday, Ally girl." Peering up at me through watery eyes, she smiled.

"Thanks, Ash."

Releasing her, I looked over to where Charlie stood off to the side, holding their boy, Spencer, in her arms, bouncing him lightly. I watched as she hummed to him, letting his mama have her moment in the spotlight because, God knows, his cuteness always gets the attention of those around him. A smattering of blond hair lined the top of his head, his baby-smooth skin tan from his time in the sun this afternoon. He giggled happily as his mom lifted him above her head, blowing a raspberry on his belly. My chest warmed at the sight and, for a brief, almost fleeting moment, I wanted what they had. A family to call mine.

Someday, I told myself, someday, I'll find it.

"She's so good with him."

Ally whispered, her eyes filled with emotion as she looked at her wife as if she'd hung the mood and stars; as if she was looking at her whole world. That love that the two of them shared? I'd never felt it, but a pang of longing in my suddenly heavy chest told me I wanted to one day.

"You happy?" I already knew the answer as she looked back over to Charlie and her son, her smile one of complete and utter contentment.

"Yeah, big brother. I'm happy."

~

"You should have seen her face, man. Fuckin' priceless."

I laughed along with Lucas as he retold the story of how they surprised Ally and I shook my head, disappointed I didn't get to see the look of astonishment on her face when she opened the front door to yells of "Happy birthday!" and "Surprise!"

17

Looking across the room, my eyes landed on my baby sister and giving her a smirk, its followed by a shake of my head when she stuck her tongue out at me and rolled her eyes.

She might be a pain in my ass, but I was damn glad she was happy.

"You guys are such jerks. I hate surprise parties."

"Come on, sis. You know you loved it." Lucas teased, his chest still heaving with laughter.

Huffing exaggeratedly, she got off her seat and glared at all of us in annoyance as she headed back towards the house.

"I'm going to go help Ma in the kitchen. At least she doesn't tease me."

Feeling bad for being such an ass to her, especially on her birthday, I moved from my seat around the fire pit and wrapped my arms around Ally's shoulders, hugging her close while whispering in her ear.

"Sorry, sis."

"It's okay. I've long ago stopped being fazed by your asshole-ness."

Pulling slightly away from her with a grunt of disbelief, I looked down at her.

"That's not even a word, Ally."

"It is now. I made it up."

～

"You're a natural."

A low growl emanates from my chest as I opened my eyes, the leery and incomparable feeling of someone watching me tightening my muscles in awareness. When my gaze landed on none other than

18

my darling sister, watching me with amused eyes, mine narrowed.

"Sis, I love you and all, but watching me sleep is just fucking creepy."

It's only then that I remembered the tiny baby boy resting in the center of my chest, content to nap there.

"Well, look at that. Didn't think he'd ever fall asleep."

Sitting up with one hand securing his back, I heard Ally's sandal-clad feet padding over the hardwood floors of the room as she retrieved his diaper bag from the bedroom, followed by her disapproving laughter as she discovered the mess left there by hurricane Spencer. He hadn't even hit the terrible twos yet, but I knew his antics would only get worse as he got older.

After our television time last night, where we watched Cars 3, we had a food fight and for once in my youth, I hadn't inspired it. Followed by a big ole mess, a messy diaper change and our much-needed nap. Yeah, babysitting was not all it's been cracked up to be.

More like organized torture. I didn't say that to my sister, though. Truth was, I was looking forward to doing it all again.

"Was he fussy?" I absentmindedly stroked his back as I looked up in time to see Ally pulling a navy-blue onesie out of his knapsack, her eyes trained on me in concern.

"Nah. We just had an interesting way of getting' ready for bed."

"Meaning you don't know how to change a diaper."

Chuckling, I felt Spencer squirming in my hold and dropping my head to his hair, I hoped he wouldn't wake just yet. I was hoping to get the mess cleaned up before he had another go at it, at least.

"Shhh, little man. Your mama and I are talking, but you don't have to wake up just yet." My gentle whispers didn't do much, though, because his eyes popped open and a big smile told me he was ready for another day of mayhem.

Rocking my head back against the cushion with a thud, I heard Ally snort.

"Like I said, Ash, you're a natural."

4

TAYLA

"*A*re you okay?"

God, I was tired of hearing those three words. *Are you okay?* As if I could ever be okay after the last year of my life.

Tough didn't even begin to cover it.

Twelve months, three days and nine hours ago, I gave my heart away.

I let go of my baby boy and with him, gave up the biggest and most important piece of my heart. I wouldn't be surprised if there was a gaping hole in my chest from the loss, because that was what it felt like, everyday living without the weight of him in my stomach and the hope of his young life in my soul.

I missed him.

Every second.

Every minute.

Every day.

And I knew I'd never stop missing him. No matter how hard I had worked over the past sixty days in the rehab center my brother found for me. Bettering myself as I found ways to keep my head above water, the constant craving for the ecstatic high of the needle I loved so much at bay. I could have stayed locked up in these white, sanitary walls for the rest of my young life and I still wouldn't be deserving of that beautiful little boy that, at one time, I'd called my son.

Getting pregnant was never part of my plan. I was a planner, always had been. I didn't know how to be anything else. My entire life was a series of choices, ones that I took great care in making.

I was supposed to finish high school, go to community college in Austin and commute back and forth so that I was able to stay at home and help my mom run her flower shop. I would get a degree in business so I could take over for her when she retired in a few years and go back to school once I had someone to manage the day to day stuff for me.

My mom had always been my best friend, my confidant and my supporter through everything life through my way. Even when I met Trent and went down the wrong path, she'd never once judged me or said a harsh word.

She'd just loved me and pushed me to get help, time and time, again. My planned-out life had gone to shit as soon as I met Trent and took the first hit from a needle he gave me.

Try it, he said. It's not a big deal.

And like the stupid, young girl I was, I let him push that needle into my arm. I let him make that choice for me, because I was tired. So tired of feeling like I was the broken, unlovable girl he made me believe I was.

I was tired of classes that I couldn't keep up in, homework lasting well into the night, even though I had to be up at eight to do it, all over again.

I was tired of being the good girl with the perfect grades and the smile on her face, always needing to make sure everybody else was okay when inside I was crumbling in on myself. And that was where my addiction begun.

When I missed my period, I told myself it wasn't a big deal. I couldn't be pregnant. *I just couldn't.*

I wasn't ready. I wanted a family, more than anything in the world. But raising a baby without a career to support him or a place to call my own was foolish, reckless and most of all stupid on my part.

I wouldn't bring a baby into the darkness of my world, I wouldn't be selfish with an innocent life, one that didn't deserve to grow up with a mother like me. *I had to let him go.*

When my daddy met Charlie at one of his home renovation jobs, it was like a sign from God. He'd sent us two good and loving people that were more than willing to take in my unforeseen miracle and give him a home that I didn't have. Give him a *life* I couldn't give him.

He was always meant to be theirs, even if losing him meant I wouldn't ever feel truly whole again.

"I'm scared." I'd said those two words plenty of times in my time in rehab. My older brother, Blake worried himself silly over the past year and when he'd told me to go, I didn't want to give in. I wanted to let the darkness and the high take me under until all I could feel was that sweet, sweet nothingness.

But Blake was a relentless and stubbornly dedicated man. He wouldn't take no for an answer and eventually, I submitted to his wishes. Because he was family. Because I was losing control.

Because I was tired of wanting the darkness.

And most of all, because I wanted to bask in the light again. I couldn't keep the need for the high at bay anymore.

I was an addict. Those words were the hardest part of my recovery, without any doubt.

Admitting I needed help meant so much more than a measly few word.

Oh, no. It meant I wasn't okay. And that stubbornness my brother had? I had it, tenfold. With time, I came to terms with my addiction and nevertheless, I was still here. I was *alive.*

And I was healthy, for the first time since my boy's birth.

Take it one day at a time. It will get easier.

Heard those words plenty of times, too. Too bad it was way easier to say them, than to live the meaning of them.

"You're ready, Tayla. You have the tools we've given you and the support system behind you to stay sober. You've got this."

I nodded, hugging Dr. Sloane extra tight since I knew it would most likely be the last time we'd see each other, though I hoped we'd keep in touch by email. Leaving this place meant relying solely on myself and my meetings on keeping me sober and healthy, away from the dark place my life had been before walking in here. I couldn't let anything get in the way of that.

I knew fixing myself was my number one priority, as it should be.

Dating and romance would inevitably figure into my life, but my sobriety was my focus now. *It had to be, if I had any hope of staying me.*

"Stay in touch, okay? Please don't be a stranger, Tayla."

Holding onto her warm, too comforting embrace for a few more moments, I nodded while wiping at my leaking eyes. I was pretty sure I'd never cried as much as I had in the last two months.

Getting clean would do that to you.

"Ready?" Peeling away from one another, I nodded, sudden hope welling up inside of me at the promise of finally leaving this place.

"Yeah. I think I am."

~

"*Shit,* it's good to see you."

The very second Blake's warm yet comfortingly strong arms surrounded my waist, I burst into tears. All of my strength seemed to drain from me as he held me with a tight hold I hoped he would never release me from. I buried my nose into the collar of the light blue shirt he wore and at the first whiff of my big brother's aftershave, I was able to breathe through it.

Right there, in his arms, his presence, with his soft murmurs of reassurance next to my ear, I was able to find my strength again. I realized something in the fleeting moments when he held me, this man who never strayed, never gave up on me, never lost sight of the person I *was,* as well as the person he knew I *could* be.

I realized right then that I was strong enough.

To stay clean.

To find myself again.

To be *okay.*

And it meant everything to me.

More than a promise, more than any gift he could have and most likely would have given me. No, this reassurance meant more.

With him in my corner, my family, my meetings— I could make it through.

"I'm s—sorry, Blake."

"Shh, I know, I know. You don't have to apologize anymore, not to me."

Begrudgingly, I separated myself from his hold and nodded, felt the warm sensation of him kissing the top of my head while one of his large, muscular arms circled my shoulders, keeping me close even as I attempted to move far enough to reach his gaze.

"I have a lot of apologies to make, B."

"Yeah, you do, T. But I'm not one of them, got it?" Nodding, I let him lead me away, toward what would come next, my new life that began today.

My new normal. It was what I'd wanted for so long.

A fresh start. So, why was I so afraid of it?

~

"Tayla!" My sister's ecstatic voice carried over the front yard of my childhood home as I stepped down from the Jeep and smiled for the first time in way too fucking long.

"Scar."

"*Tay.*" We fell into a clinch that was just as soul-baring and healing as my reunion with Blake had been, even more so since I knew that, unlike my brother, she knew the depths of my struggle with temptation. My sister was an ER nurse and loved her job, but she was a recovering alcoholic and struggled with her sobriety just as much as I was sure I would in the coming months.

The day-to-day battle with her craving for alcohol stemmed from the grueling nature of her job and the havoc it played on her heart, especially when experiencing a loss. Though I'd watched her go through it all, it sadly hadn't stopped me from finding my own fix.

I'd chosen most likely the worst substance I could put into my body and I did it willingly, just for that rapturous high. To be numb, unfeeling, *invisible*.

I hoped, in time, I would be able to think of that same high and feel nothing.

No twitch of the eyes. No heat through the veins. No buzz of desperation within my mind.

Until then, I would hold onto the ones I loved. They were my support now and with them, I would get there.

"I'm so sorry I couldn't be there to pick you up. Tyler got home today." Scarlet whispered as she wrapped her arms around my neck and squeezed me tight.

God. I had missed so much. Tyler, her husband, was a marine and had been away for the past six months, with a few meager phone calls and texts between them as means of communication.

Scarlet missed him like crazy, I knew that from our nightly talks while I'd been inside. *I was so happy for her.*

"Of course I understand, sis. Is he here? I'd love to say hi."

"Hey, little sis." The deep, gravelly tone of a voice behind me had me spinning quickly around and I smiled at the big man standing just a few feet away, tattooed, burly arms crossed over his chest and a wry grin painted across his face, one I was sure was the reason my sister fell so deeply and so quickly for him.

"Hey, you." I was quickly swept up into one of his signature bear hugs. His strong yet always gentle arms bound around my torso while hoisting me off of my feet as a sweet kiss landed on the top of my head, something most of the men in my family made a habit of around my sister and I. They were all these largely built military men, but what most people didn't know was that they were all softies underneath the hard shell and tribal ink. It was both endearing and annoying as hell.

"We fuckin' missed you, Tayla." Sniffing away the sudden need to cry against his black t-shirt, I nodded.

"I'm home, now."

"Yeah." He grinned even wider, slowly releasing me and looking me over, making sure I was alright. The men in my family made that a custom, too.

Always so concerned, so attentive, so *good*.

They'd all gotten those traits from my daddy.

At the reminder, I looked past Tyler and Scarlet standing in front of me, past the ample rose bushes lining the front yard and patio and to the front door of my childhood home.

"He's not here." Blake was the first one to pick up on my worry and my eyes flashed quickly up to his, immediately concerned that the damage I'd done was too much for him to move past. My dad was just as stubborn and hard-headed as the rest of us and if he was mad enough, he could avoid me for much longer than today.

Call me selfish, but I wasn't sure I could do this without him.

He was my dad. My anchor. My biggest cheerleader and best ally.

How could I be whole, again without him?

How could he?

5

TAYLA

"Mom?" I rounded the corner of the kitchen, painted a pretty yellow and decorated with little touches of my mothers country charm everywhere. My mom was standing at the large, granite island that separated the kitchen and dining room, her hands busy cutting up a salad and an apron wrapped around her waist that read *Best Mom Ever*. And she really was the best.

The woman had given me everything – love, safety, friendship; what had I given her in my darkest hours?

Angry words and forgotten loyalty.

Unjustified blame and slanted avoidance.

You hurt the ones closest to you the most.

The saying was true when it came to us. She'd been the easiest target for my pain and grief at a time when it was all I could see.

"Mom." I said her name again, watching her shoulders tense as I neared, the anxiety she was feeling filling the space between us.

What if she couldn't forgive me?

What if she told me to leave?

My heart felt as if it dropped to my stomach at the thought and tears welled in my eyes as I counted the seconds it took for her petite frame to turn towards me.

Our closely knit bond was the very first bridge I burned after falling prey to my high, pushing her out of my life with no regard for her feelings, all because of the numbness I chased, craving it more than anything in the world.

How could I have been so stupid?

"You're..." I didn't know what I expected her to say or to do when she finally laid her eyes on me, but the sight of her wide, hazel eyes, just like mine, filling with tears wasn't one of them. She shook her head gently, as if she couldn't believe I was standing in front of her. *I wish I'd never left, Mom.*

"*Thank you. God, thank you.*" Warm, harboring arms wrapped around my waist while her voice whispered in my ear, the sound of a prayer settling around us, giving me hope that it would all be okay.

A crushing sob that I didn't know I'd been holding inside left me as I clung desperately to my mother's small frame, hoping she knew just how much I'd missed this.

Her. This. Home.

"Oh, my sweet girl. You've come back to us." Her arms cocooned me in their warmth as she squeezed me and it felt as if every second of my recovery was worth it. Because I was back where I belonged and this moment was all that mattered.

"I wish I'd never left, Mom."

"Then, stay." Simple as that, she drew back from the embrace, one of her pale hands going to my cheek in a loving touch I'd felt hundreds of times before. I knew she didn't mean just for the party, tonight. No, she wanted her little girl back home with her and more than anything, I wanted that.

I just wanted to be home, again.

"I'm sorry, Mom. You'll never know how much I wish I could change things."

"I know, baby. I know. It's all going to be okay, now."

Nodding, I dropped my head to hers, hoping she knew just how much I regretted causing her so much grief.

I've been a terrible daughter.

"I'm proud of you. We all are."

Lifting my eyes again to hers, so similar to mine, I felt the brimming tears filling my eyes.

I don't deserve her.

"Mom..."

"I know you don't think you deserve it and trust me, I understand the feeling. But you made a choice to get better and to find the help you needed. It wasn't easy, it wasn't the easy way out. Some people never find the inner strength you have running through you, every time you resist the urges I know you live with, now. You're stronger than me, baby. Please, believe that."

"*Mom.*" It was me that went into her arms this time and as I bound my body around hers, swaying gently as we cried together, I knew where I'd gotten my strength from.

It was this woman, right here. She was the strongest person I knew and if I was even a fraction of the woman she was, I considered myself lucky.

"I love you, Mom."

"I love you, too. Always. Now, come help me with dinner."

~

"You know we don't need this much food, right?"

I knew the second she heard about Blake's record deal, she would want to throw a celebratory dinner. It's what she always did when one of us had made her proud. He'd told me all about it on the ride over her and though it hurt that I'd missed such a big moment in his life, I was just happy I'd be here to celebrate with him, now.

Moving her attention from the large egg salad she'd been prepping for tonight's get together, my mom raised a thin eyebrow at me.

"Mom. You could feed an army with all this food."

"Have you ever known me to do anything half-way?" Shaking my head, I reached into the food pantry to grab more ingredients, keeping in the smirk that threatened to spread.

"There is a such thing as moderation. I mean, we have three courses of food here. It's going to be wasted, Mom." Waving a nonchalant hand in my direction, she simply added a bit more lettuce to the salads we prepped for tonight and threw a dishrag my way.

"Blake and his friends will finish it, I'm sure. Wipe down here while I wrap all of this up, alright?" Nodding, I just grinned, secretly loving our easy banter after going so long, without it.

It felt damn good to be home.

Closing the refrigerator only seconds later,

empty-handed, my mom looked me up and down a few times, her assessing eyes sweeping over me before concern etched her expression.

"You look tired." I was exhausted, whether from the emotionally draining day I'd had or the lack of sleep the night before, I wasn't entirely sure.

But having this time with her was worth the fatigue I felt throughout my body.

"Mom, I'm..."

"Come on, I'll help you get settled in. I know you're fine, but sleep won't hurt." Instead of arguing with her, like I'd planned, I nodded, not wanting to disturb our time together with as silly an argument as this one.

"Okay, you're probably right. My bags are still in Blake's car, though."

"I'm sure he won't mind grabbing them for you. Blake, honey!"

My brother's head popped into the kitchen doorway a moment later and I laughed softly to myself. She had him wrapped around her finger and she knew it.

"What's up, Ma?"

"Would you grab Tayla's things? She's going to go up for some sleep before the party." Moving farther into the doorway, he shook his head at her, hitting her with an annoyed look.

"I thought you said it would be a small gathering, Ma." Hands on her hips, she huffed as if he was being crazy.

"How am I supposed to show you off with only a few people in attendance? And anyways, you never go out, honey. It's up to me to find you a nice girl, God knows you're not looking."

Throwing his head back, my brother sighed dramatically.

"I don't need another one of your set-ups, Ma. I'm a grown-ass man and..."

"And you can live your own life, yeah, yeah, I know."

Chuckling at her sassy comments, he moved into the room and leant his head down to kiss her forehead, muttering under his breath.

"Love you, Ma."

"Go on. She needs to get settled in."

"I'm going, I'm going."

As he left the house, I peeked a glance at my mom, surprised to see an indulgent smile spread over her features.

My mom, the matchmaker.

God, help us all.

I was still laughing when he came back into the room, carrying my bags and as I followed him upstairs, I bumped his shoulder with mine.

"She really wants you to meet someone, huh?"

"You have no fucking idea, T."

"Just bring a date tonight. She'll leave you alone."

"Nah. If it makes her happy, I don't mind it." Setting my suitcases down at the door to my childhood bedroom, he pulled me into his chest, holding me close for a few minutes before gently patting my back.

"Do you want me to stay with you for a while?"

"No, it's okay. I'm just going to rest my eyes for a bit. Thanks, though."

Releasing me, he nodded, kissing my cheek and closing the door behind him, as he left.

Letting out a long, relieved breath, I felt peace for

the first time in months and I knew, without a doubt, it was because I was here, in this place.

Quickly shedding my blouse, jeans and bra, I slipped an oversized tee over my head, crawled under the covers of the soft, welcoming bed and fell asleep almost instantly.

6

TAYLA

"*You want a hit, love?*"

Shaking my head, I felt the buzz of the high that seeped through my veins lessen with each second that passed.

Trent outstretched one of his hands, a joint lodged between the gap of his long, slim, fingers and a knowing smile plastered over his lips.

He knew I'd cave.

The rush just one hit would give me far outweighed anything else, including my promises to stay clean.

I took the hit every time I attempted more than a few hours of sobriety and it didn't matter what he offered, weed, pills I was up for it all.

But H was a different story. I would do anything for a jab, one little sting of the power it possessed. It was my drug, my weakness and at times, my worst vice.

Completely, solely, irrefutably.

Shooting myself up with that blissful substance did something to me, deep inside. It let me be free. Free of the sadness I lived with daily, free from the anguish, *the loneliness, even the soul-crushing grief that inhabited my heart, now.*

And I was desperate in my need for it.

Trent knew that, too.

Looking over at him, I scooted back from the meager personal space he'd gained on me, disallowing me even that distance from my cravings.

"Yeah, I... need one."

My voice cracked, throat dry from lack of water, though I was sure the bottle of Smirnoff I'd been nursing all day hadn't helped its state.

"Bet you do, baby. You know I'll always take care of you."

It was his way of ensuring his hold on me and, like the foolish, desperate woman I'd become, I let him.

Taking a long, slow pull from the joint he'd given me, I let the world around me fade away as the buzz of the high sung through my veins.

"Mom?" Suddenly, the room around me that had been spinning turned still, the sound of the music coming from the hotel room behind us faded away; all I heard was that small, singular sound of a young child's voice.

Never heard it before in my life, but somehow, I knew it.

Deep in my bones, in my heart, in my soul, if I even possessed one.

"Mom? What are you doing?"

He couldn't be a day older than two, but boy, had he grown.

A full head of shaggy light brown hair, thick strands of it falling across his face as he looked at me with big, hazel eyes, just like mine.

God, he was beautiful. He looked just like me.

Or at least, the girl I used to be.

Innocent.

Beautiful.

Young.

"Why aren't you around, Mom? I need you."

Attempting to stand, I grabbed Trent's arm, hoping, no, praying, for a helping hand.

I just needed to hold him. Just a minute with him would be enough.

My boy. My beautiful, little boy.

He was growing up so fast and I wasn't there for even a moment of it.

The realization of that truth caused what felt like a knife penetrating my heart, creating a larger hole where he belonged.

Where he'd always belong.

"Baby, I'm sorry –"

"Where you goin', baby? You're mine, now. He's not even yours anymore."

Trent smiled down at me, standing at his full height, his hollow laugh filling the room and instead of the sudden warmth and love I'd felt for my son, I felt hatred.

Hatred of myself. Hatred of my addiction. Hatred of him.

"He will always be mine." *I didn't care what I had to do, I could be his mom again, I vowed to myself and moved my gaze back to my boy, only to see empty space.*

He'd left me. He was... gone.

Again.

"Spencer!"

"*Wake up*, sunshine. Wake up, now."

The hushed whispers of a strong, deep voice

pulled me out of my dreams in an instant, my heart calling out to that voice, one I hadn't heard in way too long.

"Hey, come here. I'm here now. It's all going to be okay. It's alright."

My body shook in the aftermath of the dream, one I hadn't had in weeks and one that left me reeling. It had felt so real, so vivid, I couldn't help but wonder if it was like an omen; was it the universe's way of telling me that I still hadn't *truly* let go of Spencer, as if I ever could?

Physically, I had to. But emotionally, I still felt him.

"Daddy—" Pulling me tightly into his arms, my father peered down at me with a solemn look on his face, concern and ever—present love emanating from his gaze.

I missed him so much.

The fear and unease from my dream begun slowly fading, the longer I sat in the circle of my father's arms. It was the one and only place that had always felt safe to me, secure. Nothing would hurt me with him near. I knew that deep in my heart.

"I'm so sorry I wasn't here, Sweetheart. I was being stubborn, giving you tough love. I should have been here when you got home, I shouldn't have stayed away."

Moving my head from his chest and hooking my arms around his neck, I shook my head at him, unwilling to let him blame himself when I should have been the one apologizing for all the ways I'd let him down, time and time again.

"I understood, Dad. I promise, it's okay." Shaking

his head in disbelief, he pulled me in closer, pressing a kiss to the top of my head before speaking again.

"What did you dream about?"

"*Spencer.*" My breath got caught in my throat as I spoke his name, as it always did when my thoughts went to the past year of my life, to the day I gave him up, the day that changed my life and his, forever.

He would have a happy, healthy life with the family I chose for him, but I couldn't help but feel saddened that that life wouldn't include me.

I'll never be a part of his life, no matter how much I yearn to be.

"I still miss him. It hurts so much, to think of him, to *miss* him. What do I do, Dad? When will it stop hurting?" Tears pooled heavily beneath my eyes and I blinked, allowing them to fall onto my cheeks, more following their wake. My heart squeezed tightly within my chest as I struggled to breathe through the splicing of my lungs, caused by my deep-seated longing for a son that was never truly mine.

I would give anything to have him back, though.

"I don't know, sweetheart. You've experienced a loss I don't think I'd ever be able to handle. Losing you or your siblings would break me, I'm not gonna lie about that. I would probably find the nearest bottle and get lost at the bottom of it, rather than deal with the pain of losing any of you. But, you're not doing that, are you?"

His confession rocked me to my core, because showing his emotions was something I'd only heard from my dad a few times in my life and I knew his admittance of them was not an easy one. His question rolled around my mind for a few minutes before I could answer and when I did, I realized why he'd asked it, in the first place.

"I lost myself, Dad. I don't even know where to go from here."

"You start over. You take it one step, one day at a time and when things get hard, you lean on those around you. Your mom, me, Scarlet and Blake. Your friends. Your meetings. That's what we're all here for, Tayla. To help you."

Nodding, I let his words seep through my skin, permeate my heart and strengthen my resolve.

"I love you, Dad." I felt him kiss my head again as exhaustion weighted my eyelids and the solace our talk had given me warmed my heart.

"I love you . Always remember that."

It was the last thing I heard before I submitted to a deep and thankfully dreamless sleep.

7

ASHER

"*Y*ou never told me you lived in a mansion, man."

Blake turned into his family's home and slowed to a stop on a plot of perfectly cut grass. On the drive there, I saw miles and miles of farmland and cattle grazing and it felt like I had stepped into an episode of *Little House On The Prairie*. I knew his family owned a small horse farm but this was nowhere near what I'd been expecting. Maybe a nice house with a few acres of land, just big enough for a horse stable and grass for them to roam.

But this was not small in any sense of the word.

"We've added on and bought more land in the last few years. We had humble beginnings, though and it wasn't always easy. We made do with what we had at the time and now that I'm making more with my music, I hope I can help my parents live more comfortably. You'll love them, they're good people."

"It sure is impressive, Blake. If they are half as cool as you are, I'm sure we'll get along fine." Grinning, he opened the front door to the house for me and followed me in. The first things I saw were the spacious living-slash-dining room and a short, blonde woman who had to be Blake's mother, Katherine.

"You must be Mrs. Reynolds. Thank you for having me."

I leant in and planted a gentle kiss on her cheek and she smiled, bright and beautiful; from ear to ear. A lot about her reminded me of my own mother and my chest seized with memories of kissing her goodbye after each one of my visits home. Sometimes, they sneaked up on me, reminders of her. I breathed through the fucking impossible pain in my chest and smiled back at her, taking her hand in mine when she reached for it. I could tell, just from meeting her, that she was just as much of a kind soul as Blake was, if not more so.

They're just good people and that shit was rare, nowadays. Sad, but true.

"You must be hungry. Come on in, there's plenty of food. Blake here hasn't been much help."

"Ma!" He crossed his arms over his chest, feigning annoyance with this sweet woman he called mom but I saw the amusement in his eyes.

"Hush, you." She slapped his arm, scolding him in the way all mothers do.

She winked at the pair of us before hooking her arm in one of mine and led the way to the equally spacious kitchen of her home, the fucking delicious scent of whatever she was cooking wafting through the air.

A man could get used to this.

"Look who's here, Jackson." I turned my head to see who she had her eyes trained on and saw a tall, older man who I guessed was Blake's father.

"Good to see you made it, Asher. I hope you brought an appetite."

Nodding, I shook his hand firmly, noticing the evident muscle mass held in his forearms and broad shoulders. It was a hint of how well he took care of himself, even in retirement.

"You can bet on it, sir." We settled ourselves in the living room as Katherine cooked in the kitchen, while the rest of the family gathered by the terrace, catching up on each other's lives with conversation and laughter I could hear through the open patio door. Making small talk about music, life and family, the time flew by before I heard a sweet voice call from the doorway of the kitchen.

"This food's going to get cold, boys. Come and get it!"

As we cleared the sliding glass door on the side of the house, I saw the long, wooden picnic tables set up for dinner, and the happy, smiling faces of Blake's family and friends surrounding us. I thought I would feel out of place, being around a family that wasn't mine, but I was anything but. From the second I stepped into the house, I was welcomed with open arms and kind hearts. Sitting down by one end of the table, I grinned at Blake as he settled in beside me, surprisingly thankful for him bringing me here, even if I'd been unsure, at first.

"They're really great, man. Thank you for having me."

"I'm glad you're here, Asher. My mom already loves you."

I nodded, smiling widely. The gruff sound of Jackson's voice pulled in my attention and drew me away from the surprising kindness these strangers had shown me.

"Has anyone seen Tayla? She should have come down by now..."

My gaze moved from him to an empty chair a few chairs down from mine, only then realizing we were missing someone.

Blake stood beside me, the same concern I saw in his father's eyes painted over his expression. Gone was the carefree, happy man I was just chatting with. He was a concerned brother now and, being part of a large family myself, I completely got it.

You can't help but feel worry for those you love, it's like instinct. It's immediate and unavoidable.

I watched him rush back into the house and my gut tightened, a sinking feeling settling deep inside of me as we waited for him to find his sister and all I could do was hope all was okay. Knowing some of her struggles from what Blake had confided in me, I knew how much he worried about her and the thought of anything bad happening to her was like a kick to my stomach.

I wondered why I even cared. *I'd never even met the girl.*

Unlike my brothers, I'd always worn my heart on my sleeve, wanting everyone around me to be happy even if inside I was anything, but. My mom used to call me *tootsie* because she believed that, though I was hard on the outside, with a shell to protect me from the world around me, inside I was complete goo.

I blinked a few times to rid myself of the sudden mist that had formed beneath my eyes at the memory and was saved from any more of my reminiscent thoughts when I heard large, booted footsteps leaving the house and walking toward us, followed by the lighter footsteps of his sister. Relief went through the room around me even as my gut clenched tightly once more, except this time it wasn't out of worry or misplaced concern.

Feeling the hairs at the back of my neck stand on end, I was suddenly acutely focused on the sound of her approaching and looking down at my plate, I mentally berated myself; unsure why I was suddenly so focused on a woman I'd never even met.

Look up, my mind told me.

Look at her.

My heart beat just a little faster.

God, she's beautiful. My eyes, hungry and ravenous, curious and spellbound, swept from the tips of her toes, toenails painted a sunny yellow color, in the brown sandals she wore and I let my gaze wander. Up, up, up her long, toned calves, noticing the little freckles on her legs as I admired them. Trim little waist, hips with just enough meat for me to grab onto, as I loved to do. I was a man of many tastes and those perfect hips were one of them. She had the best love handles I'd ever laid my eyes on and I was fucking salivating at the sight.

Hearing voices around me, I was pulled from the spell her fucking perfect body had captured me in when I heard my name.

"Asher, meet my baby sister, Tayla. Sis, this is Asher. He's my producer at the record company I've been working with."

Standing quickly, I moved closer to them, hoping for the chance to touch her, just once. I had no idea what was going on with me right then, why I was suddenly so interested in this girl... this girl I knew hadn't had it easy in her young life. I'd heard enough from her brother to know that something had caused her to fall into depression and inevitably, her addiction to hardcore drugs. I'd barely tried any of it, myself, so the idea of her having a taste of it had me on high alert, the protective side of me rearing its head and I didn't even know her name.

When you know, you know.

My father's words came back to me, shadowing through my mind like a truth I didn't want to face. I didn't even know this girl's name, and I wanted her.

It was something my dad would often tell my brothers and me when we asked him for advice with women. He said that the first time he saw our mom, he knew he would marry her. At the time, I thought he was completely nuts, but now, as I took in the blonde bombshell in front of me, I wasn't so sure.

I stopped directly in front of them, only a breath and a step away from her and I was finding it hard to breathe. The scent of cherries hit my nose, the sweet smell emanating off of her in waves and I was losing myself.

Big, hazel eyes trapped me, holding me captive and I couldn't look away, even if I'd wanted to. *Fuck, no I don't want to.*

She had a mouth painted ruby red, plump and full and *perfect* to fit just right around the head of my cock that had become steel in her presence. Never really liked blondes, but this one, this gorgeous little thing, was lethal to my self-control.

I knew next to nothing about her but I was damn sure of one thing; she was a game-changer.

"Hi." Her voice, honey and silk, hit my ears and all I could think was, *I want you.* I wasn't so sure that would go over very well so I came up with something else to say.

"Hi, back, Tayla Reynolds."

I watched in rapturous fascination as a scarlet blush covered her cheeks. Her eyes dropped from mine as she fiddled with the rings on her fingers and, for a split second, I was worried she may be married. But, as I looked at her hands – pale, thin fingers painted to match her toes – I was relieved to see no wedding or engagement rings.

Not even a ring would keep me from wanting her, though.

I was pretty sure that truth wouldn't go over so well, either. Reaching for her hands, I glided my fingers through hers and lifted both hands to my mouth, where I planted a chaste kiss on each.

Much better than a handshake, if I do say so myself.

I was almost tempted to wink at her, yet resisted, unsure of how she felt about meeting me, or if she was open to my flirting ways.

I'd always had good luck with women, but suddenly, all of that didn't matter to me. I just wanted to get to know her. The real Tayla. Not the addict, but the daughter, the sister, the friend. I wanted every damn part of her, if she'd let me.

Knowing I wouldn't say any of that right then, I just gave her a grin and released her, watching as her eyes stayed on mine even after I released her hands.

That's right, Angel. Keep your eyes on me.

And she did, all through dinner with her all—too —welcoming family and her brother's watchful eyes on me, all the while.

Jesus, she's fucking beautiful.

8

TAYLA

The way he looked at me scared me. As if he was searching my heart with those penetrating, blue eyes of his, the look in his eyes telling more than his words could say.

I've never seen a look like this one from anyone and if I was honest, I was pretty tempted to run away from that look. Call me crazy, but Asher Jones seemed like just the type of man who would break my heart and not even know he was doing it.

He was just that smooth, that hot, that irresistible. But I could resist him.

Right?

"Why do you look at me like that?" *Crap!* I'd said that out loud.

Stupid girl, what are you doing?

One of two things would happen. Either he would say something that made me want him even more than you I already did, or he'd say something that'd make no sense, until it was too late.

Men do that a lot, you know. They made no sense until you're under them and by that time, I'd have no hope of resisting him.

If my relationship with Trent, the very reason for my battle with my addiction, taught me anything, it was that I had crap judgment when it came to the opposite sex. I wouldn't know a good man if he was thrown my way. Because I'd thought, with my whole heart that Trent was right for me and I was oh, so wrong, wasn't I?

So, when Asher leant his head to the side, dark strands of his hair falling into his eyes, I knew I shouldn't have stepped just a little closer to him. I only met him a few short hours ago and I was already unable to look away.

I hadn't been this attracted to a man in... *ever*. But would I admit that to him? *Hell no.*

"Because you're a fucking angel, Tayla. I'm not that guy, you know. The one who falls at a woman's feet, begs for scraps, calls them baby and wants a fairytale. I'm the man that you don't bring home to your mother. The man that your father fears you'll end up with. The rebel. The bad boy. That's me, Tayla. But you, *fuck*, I don't know. I just want to know more."

My breath got trapped in my throat at his softly spoken confession – well, as softly spoken as his deep, raspy baritone could be. His rough tone and insistent demeanor should have scared me, at-least scared me enough to stay away from him. But it didn't, not even a little bit.

I could give in to temptation for one night, right? And tomorrow I could go back to my lonely existence, making amends for all the bridges I'd succeeded in burning. Because, let's face it, I wasn't a damsel in distress and he wasn't my prince, coming to save me.

I was tainted. Broken.

Hard to love. Damaged goods.

But sex... sex was something I'd be up for with him. The bad boy, as he called himself. I wasn't entirely sure he was right about that, not by the way my brother spoke about him, but I didn't dare say that.

"More?" I found myself whispering, pulled closer by the intensity in his gaze, the sexy way he grinned and bit his lip making *me* want more.

"Yeah, more." He leaned in close, only my slice of apple custard pie keeping us apart. It was my favorite dessert, hands down, but right then? I hated that I was holding it.

Because if I wasn't...

"I want to touch you where no one else has. I want to lick every fucking inch of your skin and discover all your hidden freckles. That's more, Tayla. So, tell me. What do you want?"

I heard the challenge in his voice, in the panty-melting smile spreading his mouth. I'd never imagined wanting someone again after what my last relationship had resulted in. I couldn't say I had trust issues.

Oh, no. I had issues, period. Self-love issues. Men issues. Intimacy wasn't my strong suit, never had been. Sex? Well, I hadn't had much of it but what I did, wasn't much to write home about.

Turns out the jerk of a junkie I'd dated was not the best lover. Who knew?

I definitely hadn't, but, at a time in my life where I had yearned for something other than soul-crushing loneliness and consuming depravity, I gratefully took the small amount of closeness Trent offered me.

I wasn't supposed to date until I hit the six month

mark in my sobriety journey, as Dr. Sloan so nicely described it.

I just called it surviving.

I felt Asher's long, thick fingers glide over my wrists, one hand taking my dessert plate from my grasp. As he placed it behind me on the kitchen island, it was like I'd lost the ability to breathe.

All I could feel were his hands, on my wrists, holding me firmly in his grasp. It was a threatening touch, one that should have waved all kinds of red flags in my mind, yet it had the opposite effect all together. The instantaneous feeling of being protected, of being held, squeezed my chest and warmed my body, all over. Goosebumps that trailed over my skin were a giveaway of just how much I wanted his touch, even if my mind told me not to.

"I want to *kiss* you, Angel." That name, again. I'd never really liked pet names with the guys I'd dated before, but with him?

Just the sound of his name for me had me wanting him, even more.

From somewhere deep inside of me, my fight or flight instincts kicked in.

And I ran.

On trembling legs and with a softly muttered apology on my lips, I fled the kitchen and quickly mounted the stairs leading to my bedroom, both hoping he'd chase me and wishing he'd let me be.

I should have known better than to wish for the latter.

~

Knock, knock.

Rolling onto my side, I told myself I was hearing things. After coming upstairs and taking a nice, hot shower, I crawled in here and never left.

"You can run, Angel, but I'll chase you. I'm not afraid of a little chase."

God, no.

He was right there, behind my door. He'd *found* me. *Why?*

I sat up and pushed my feet back into my sandals, grateful that I'd put on a pair of leggings and one of my long shirts I often wore to bed before heading in for the night.

Opening my door, I wasn't entirely sure how I felt about Asher being in my bedroom but knew I had to face him. He was a part of Blake's life and even if I ran from him now, I'd have to face him, eventually.

"Fuck, look at you." Looking down at my outfit, I frowned, the sudden spark of insecurity tightening my stomach at his words.

I'd taken my makeup off after coming upstairs, wanting to sleep more than anything else. I normally didn't even bother wearing it, but tonight had been special. It was my first time seeing everyone after so long away and I just wanted everybody to see that I was okay, now. They didn't have to worry about me, anymore.

But it hadn't just been them I wanted to impress. After meeting Asher, I realized I was longing for the love I knew my sister had. The love my parents still shared. And although I knew I wasn't deserving of it, I still wondered if in another life, Asher and I would have had it. And a small, lonely part of me wanted him to like me even half as much I knew I liked him.

"No, no, shit. Look at me." His voice was low and

soft, as if I was something special. His rough, callused fingers rubbed over my cheek, sending sparks of warmth all throughout my body. His eyes were on me as my heart sped in my chest, a mixture of fear and excitement thrumming through my veins.

"God, you're beautiful. Tell me you want this, Tayla. Tell me it's not just me." Nodding my agreement, I leant into his touch upon my cheeks, unable to stop my body's natural and undeniable need for him, the intensity of it all seemingly unreal.

It didn't matter that he could and most likely would hurt me, whether by breaking my heart or by his hands. It would be worth the risk, just to be his, for one night. For the first time in my life, I knew that I was safe in the arms of a man, this man. *Asher*.

And I let myself fall.

9

ASHER

*F*uck, she was sexy. Long, blonde hair, thick and wavy from her shower, cascaded over her small shoulders and those breasts... Goddamn, I couldn't keep my eyes off her for more than a second.

She had the most perfect tits I'd ever seen. Plump and round, perfectly shaped to my hands. *How was I going to resist her?*

I couldn't, that was the problem.

One look at her and every other woman in the room didn't fuckin' exist. And those lips, they were something else. Full and red, enticing me to sink my teeth into them. Actually, now that I'd thought about it, there wasn't one thing about her I didn't like. If I had to pick one, it was her shyness.

She had this tendency to shy away from attention, from praise or compliments and I had a pretty good idea as to why. She was self-conscious. It was ridiculous to me, because this little thing was awe-inspiring. I knew saying that to her wouldn't make her believe it, though. Naw, that would take some time.

I couldn't help wondering if she'd let me in if

given that time and then wanted to yell at that very thought. I was *not* a forever kind of man.

And from hearing of her struggles, her troubled past and witnessing her beautiful, sad smile, I knew she would want that. As she damn well should. She deserved it. The house and the white picket fence and the fairy-tale. She'd been hurt way too many times in her life, more than anyone should have to harbor. Her pain was evident in her pretty, hazel eyes and in the way she looked down at her hands, as if she was afraid to be seen.

I see you, Angel.

I wanted to be that man. The man to make her smile, again.

"Asher, I don't know if this is a good idea."

Her voice was like honey, smooth and buttery and I leaned in closer, only a few breaths of space between us now. Even that space was too far, in my opinion.

"Why's that, Angel?" That got her attention, those eyes of hers sparking with awareness of the name I'd begun calling her and, if the heat creeping to her cheeks didn't give it away, the way her fingers tightened on the collar of my shirt did the job.

She liked the sound of it.

"I'm not looking for love." Her admission wasn't a surprising one. This girl was freshly out of rehab after being in and out of an abusive relationship, using drugs and alcohol to numb the pain whenever she could. I would have bet money that my angel didn't know I knew about that, though. Her brother had confided in me about her, worrying about her safety every second of every day. Now, he didn't have to. Because she was with me. And I would stop at nothing to keep her safe.

At-least, for tonight.

"Ash, what do you want?"

Here goes, nothing...

"I want to *fuck* you, Tayla. I want to make you feel things you've never felt before. I want you to be mine, if only just for one night." I kissed a hot, moist trail from her earlobe to her throat, stopping at a sensitive spot on her jaw as I felt her breath halt and her body shiver in anticipation of what was to come.

Shudder for me, baby.

I was just getting started.

"I want to fuckin' stake my claim on you." Her hands, urgent and needful, wrapped my neck and held on tight, just as I wanted her.

At least for tonight.

"Yes. I— I want that, too." *Fuck yes!*

Still, I pulled back, moving my lips over the top of her head, taking the opportunity to bask in the unmistakable and intoxicating scent of her.

"Gotta be sure, Tayla. You don't have to do anything you don't want to. I like my women agreeable and if this is gonna work, I need you to want this, too."

"Asher." Just the whisper of my name off her lips and I only got harder, hotter, my cock standing to attention between us, tempting me to rub against her, just for the relief the friction would cause.

I resisted. Just barely, though.

"I want this, Asher." *Thank Christ.*

"Fuck," I breathed, her softly spoken confession breaking my self-control, my tightly held resistance of her broken, leaving me feeling unchained, beastly, *mad.*

My mouth raced over hers like I was aiming for the grand win, the tremor of lust and warmth and need rocketing through me as her peppermint taste hit my tongue.

"Fuckin' perfect..." I muttered, winding her long, golden hair around my fist and pulling just enough to make her breath cease, her eyes, wide, wild, pleading on mine as I shook my head once and forced my tongue between those pillow-soft lips of hers in my craving for another taste.

I'd never get enough. Tasting the smear of her lipstick staining my own mouth as I devoured her for the first time was heady, tongues gliding and searching, dancing and exploring, mine finding all the little spots that made her shudder, made her *feel*.

I licked along the lower cleft of her bottom lip and felt her body tense, her legs wrap around my waist in the next second as she whispered against the kiss in a fevered plea.

"Do that again."

"Gladly." This time, I added in a few gentle bites of my teeth and a hot breath and she was shaking in my arms.

Jesus, so responsive.

Soon enough, we both lost our breath, each of us chasing the heat of our connection, the electricity of our touch and the need for more that overcame everything else.

Cursing, it was like I was cutting off a limb when I removed my lips from the dessert I'd found between her lips. Begrudgingly, I did and instead, trailed my lips down her throat, licking, nipping along her skin as I went, hands securely holding her waist as she moaned and writhed, whispering my name over and over as if that would somehow save her.

I was nowhere near done with her.

Her legs hit the edge of her mattress and I moved my hands to her ass, the globes fitting just right in my hands proving my point once more. She was flawless.

I laid her down across her bed, my hands moving over her body, eager fingertips whispering over every crevice, line and dip her skin made, the smooth flesh covered in goosebumps, ones I was sure I had caused.

I liked that a hell of a lot more than I should.

Had plenty of one night stands in my life. An embarrassing amount, actually. Never before did I see the reaction *she* had to me. The way her breath halted when I touched her. The sound she made when I lowered my mouth to her jaw and nibbled at the skin, the soft moan of pleasure I pulled from her lips.

The sensation of her breath on my ear as she whispered how she couldn't think when I touched her like this, like she was the focal point of my world.

Now I did. I noticed it all.

And I didn't want to.

Shit, I shouldn't be paying attention to all these little things, the little details that made Tayla shiver, made her feel good.

But, I didn't know how to stop.

Moving my mouth to her ear, I tossed her t-shirt to the floor behind me, eyes ravishing, hungry, on her now bare flesh. Lost my ability to breathe right then.

Seeing her. I wasn't sure if she'd ever allowed a man to truly look at her before because she was instantly shy. Blushing face, darting eyes, quivering lip.

And I hated it.

You're beautiful, Angel. Don't hide it. And that's what I told her.

"You're beautiful. Never hide yourself with me, alright?"

She nodded, but her agreement with my statement didn't reach her eyes.

It was sad, but I hadn't expected it to.

Self-love wasn't so easily won. It took time, patience and love. Not only love of oneself, but love from others around her.

I didn't know much of who she was, in her heart, but what I had learned told me that she was guarded. She was afraid of being hurt, since she'd been hurt for so long, by so many people.

I didn't know how I could fix that, but in this moment I desperately wanted to.

"These freckles drive me mad," I muttered instead, my lips finding a pattern of three freckles on her pelvis, just above the line of the tiny lace panties she wore, pink, just like her flesh as I ravished it.

So. Fucking. Sexy.

"Asher." Something inside of me snapped as I lowered her panties down her long legs, smooth and shapely and *perfect*.

Needed to be inside her. My patience had run thin and my dick was done waiting. It wanted her, just as much as I did.

"Shut that pretty mouth, Angel. The only thing I want to hear from you is how good I'm making you feel. Got it?"

Nodding, she bit at her bottom lip, the hint of a teasing smile forming over her face.

"Got it."

I trailed my lips up the pale white flesh of her

thighs, letting my stubble tease her skin and entice her pleasure, only heightening the arousal she would feel when my lips met their destination. I could feel the heat of her pussy, warm and wet as I licked a hot path over her lips, earning a loud moan from her when she realized my intention.

"I've never..." Looking up at her, my hands took hold of her thighs, widening them until there was enough space for my broad shoulders to nestle between them and, as they did, I told her to hook her legs around them. There was curiosity in the depths of her hazel eyes and she eagerly moved her legs over my shoulders, connected her ankles between my shoulder-blades, earning herself another long, slow lick of my tongue. I got my first taste of her pussy and was salivating in a matter of seconds.

What the fuck was happening to me?

I couldn't remember a time I'd desired a woman like this, before, but here I was, on the edge of oblivion, desperate for one more taste of her.

One more taste would never be enough, though.

"Never been eaten out?" Shaking her head, she bit her lip again and it was enough to thrust me off the proverbial edge.

I was done taking it slow.

"Hold on tight, Angel."

10

TAYLA

The very second his mouth closed around me, I was liquefied butter underneath him.

God, those lips. That mouth.

That hungry tongue and the little bites he gave me with his teeth as he devoured me were enough to push me over the edge of sanity I'd been toeing from the moment he told me he wanted to fuck me. I didn't think resisting him was possible, the pull, the *spark*, the connection that we had was too strong. I would fight it, tomorrow. I would have to, no matter how much my feeble heart wanted more.

It just wasn't in the cards for me. I knew that. He knew that, didn't he?

I didn't have much time to think on it, not when he took the bud of my pulsing clit between his teeth and twisted the overly stimulated flesh, pulling a startled cry from my lips, while my hands, eager, desperate, fierce, were grasping onto long, dark strands of his hair in an effort to keep my footing. Being with him, like this?

It made me feel like I was spinning out of control,

losing my footing, loosening my anchor the more time we spent together, like this.

I both hated it and loved it, the way he was able to make me feel.

Beautiful. Wanted. *Sexy*.

I felt all those kinds of things in his presence and it was both amazing and exciting, a new feeling I wanted to hold onto after going for so long without the kind of emotion I felt when around this man.

But feeling these things, these unbalanced, silly emotions he inspired in me, was terrifying. Earthshaking, undeniably terrifying.

Giving myself to him was a mistake. It's what I kept trying to convince myself of. I wasn't doing a very good job of it, though.

Stupid, stupid girl.

"Need to be inside you, Angel. I can't do slow right now." His voice, deep, dark and filled with need, at my ear.

I nodded, because I couldn't deny it. How could I deny something I wanted so much?

More than my next breath.

More than any drug's hold on me. More than anything.

And I couldn't ignore it.

"Please, Asher. I need it." His lips were on mine in an instant, hot, fevered, merciless in their claim of my mouth, my lips, my *everything*.

I loved every second of it.

The tip of his erection made contact with my damp lips in the next second and I moaned loudly at the contact. The only thought in my brain was of him, just as he'd wanted all along.

This was the moment I gave my body to him.

Grabbing onto him as he pushed inside me in one smooth motion of his hips, I knew I'd never be the same.

He owned me.

11

TAYLA

*H*e owned me.

I had been right, all along.

Asher Jones had trouble written all over him, he'd even told me himself. I was pretty sure I was certifiable because I liked him, just like that. I didn't need him to be the *right man* for me. I didn't want him to be wholesome or well-rounded or be anything other than what he was.

Real. Honest. *Asher.*

My eyes fluttered opened on a sleepy yawn, my gaze traveling around my childhood bedroom before I realized just where I'd fallen asleep. And who was lying next to me, his messy brown hair having fallen over his eyes in his slumber. Turning gently onto my side in hopes of not disturbing him, I peeked up at his face, my wandering gaze taking in all of the little things about him I hadn't noticed in the throes of passion late last night.

He looked... peaceful. Like nothing and no one could touch him. Was it possible to keep a man like him? A self-proclaimed bad boy? A player of women and a musician by trade? I doubted it. It didn't stop me from yearning for it, though.

It was now or never.

Fight or flight.

Leave or stay.

I knew what I wanted to do.

It was barely dawn, I could let myself pretend that this was more than just sex. Just one night. But if I did, what would stop me from asking for more from him?

Nothing. And I couldn't take that risk.

Carefully moving his heavy arm from around my hip, I pulled my body out from underneath his, all the while hoping to be caught.

To see if he'd fight it. To see if he'd make me stay.

To hear his deep voice once more, experience his kiss, just one more time.

But, I knew that was selfish. To want more than I had to give.

What kind of person did that make me? To want him to want me, with the knowledge that all I had to offer him were the mere pieces of my heart, not a whole?

It makes you a silly girl.

Leave before it's too late.

I let out a heavy breath as I toed on my sandals and pulled some clothes from the dresser, quickly changing and hiding my bare body from his view in case he started to wake up.

I would let myself feel the loss of him when I was out of his sight and would hopefully find a way to forget last night, and this man, altogether. Lingering in the slightly open doorway of my bedroom, I doubted if it was possible to rid my memory of him, but I promised myself I would give it my best try.

What other choice did I have?

~

My chest felt like lead as I dug my cell phone out of the front pocket of my purse and hurried to find my sister's number, my feet carrying me away from home and toward my car. I hoped to God it was still kept in the garage, my little Honda I had before going into rehab this last time. Elation soared through my body as I saw it covered in a black tarp on the left side of my parents' four car garage, just as I'd remembered it. Unlocking the driver's side door, I dropped my things onto the seat and then pulled at the front of the large, plastic tarp to remove it. I wasted no time in closing the car door and putting my keys in the ignition, the first tells of a breakdown whispering through my gut and buzzing over my skin.

Having felt so many highs with Asher, followed by the low of knowing I had to leave him, was pulling my tightly-held composure apart, making it hard to focus on the road as I maneuvered onto the street, pressing on the gas with the only sense of power I had left.

I pressed my phone to my ear and, by some sort of divine intervention, she answered on the third ring. She was always there for me, whenever I needed her.

But I didn't just need her this time. I needed a meeting. Because the first thing I wanted to do after leaving Asher was shoot up, again.

"Tayla? Are you okay?"

"Y... yeah. I think so. Have breakfast with me?"

"I can come pick you up if you need me."

"No." I took a deep breath, only then realizing I'd been holding my breath.

"Okay. Are you sure you're okay? I didn't see you come back downstairs last night."

"I'll tell you everything when I get there. I'm on my way."

There was a long pause, only interrupted by the slow hum of my car's engine and the sounds of the bustling road in front of me. It was barely morning, but in downtown Austin it was rush hour. Everybody was going to work and wanted to get there quickly. That made traffic and a quick commute impossible, as I had to drive through the center of the city to get to Haven, the small town in the outskirts of Austin where my sister lived.

It left me alone with my thoughts and if I could have escaped them, I would have. Because every single thought whispering through my head contained Asher.

"Why do you look at me like that?"

"Because you're a fucking angel, Tayla."

From our night together, I knew he'd been wrong to say he was a bad boy. He'd taken care of me last night, both gentle and rough in all the right ways. And the way he'd *looked* at me? It could've made me come alone.

But still, I wasn't sure he was the type of man I was capable of handling. I needed stability, I needed someone that would be there for me, when I needed them.

One that would take care of me. One that would understand my imperfections and love me anyway.

With a job and a future and enough patience for me to wear thin.

Because, God knew, I would. Was Asher that man? My eyes clouded over with thick, unrelenting tears as I realized that I couldn't answer that.

I wanted to say no. I wanted to avoid him like the plague and write him off as a man who'd taken advantage of me, in one of my frequent weak moments.

But I couldn't do it. Because somewhere between meeting him last night and waking up in his arms this morning, I'd seen something in him that I didn't expect to see.

His heart. His protective nature that had me feeling safe for the first time in years – years of struggling with my weaknesses and wondering if I'd ever truly be whole again.

Spotting Scarlet's white house with light blue shutters on the end of the street, I pressed on the gas petal, sudden desperation to see her fueling the action. No matter the missteps I had taken in my life, she was always by my side. She was unwavering in her support and love for me and I was sure I didn't deserve it.

It didn't mean that I wouldn't accept it, because I would. She was my sister and my best friend. I couldn't do any of this without her. I just hoped she knew that.

The second I put my car into park, the front door to the house burst open, followed by my sister, her husband following closely behind. He moved his head in my direction, a soft expression of concern masked over his face. Scarlet bounded the few feet between her front yard and the driveway, her eyes on me entirely as she all but ran toward me.

I closed the car door behind me, anger at myself welling up inside me.

I hated that she was always so worried for me.

I just wanted her to be able to be happy.

I would be fine.

"Scarlet, I'm okay." Her warm, slender arms engulfed me as she hugged me tightly, not letting go even as Tyler stepped behind her and took hold of her shoulders in hopes of calming her.

"Babe. She's good. Let's go inside."

I felt her sniffling back her tears, her body holding tightly to mine. Confusion rushed through my chilled veins as my thoughts tried to piece together why she was so upset right then. I'd called her sounding upset. She had every right to feel worried and scared for me.

I knew that, but didn't know how to make it better for her. I couldn't take away her fear of losing me to my addiction. All I could do was prove to her that I wouldn't betray her trust any more than I already had.

"Are you sure you're okay?"

"I promise. I just needed some sister time. And maybe a meeting. I didn't mean to worry you." Pulling away, she turned away from me and quickly buried her face in Tyler's bare chest, grabbing hold of his forearms as his large, tanned hands settled on her back to soothe her. I heard him whisper to her and it reminded me of another man's whisper. *Asher's*.

I didn't have the faintest clue why my mind kept circling back to him, so I did what I did best. I ignored it.

As I watched them, I wondered if I'd ever find that sort of love.

Do I deserve to? I pushed those thoughts away, too.

After a few more intimate moments, Scarlet turned her eyes to mine and took my hand, squeezing my fingers with just enough pressure to tell me what I needed to know.

I love you.

Those words stayed with me as I followed her inside and settled on the leather couch in their living room, taking the large glass of water Tyler handed me.

My sister's footsteps coming down the hall grabbed my attention and, for a moment, I forgot about the intense longing that had inhabited my thoughts since leaving Asher this morning.

"I have someone who wants to meet you."

"Babe." Tyler laughed loudly, the low sound of his chuckle followed by an equally loud bark from a dog. *What the hell was that?*

A large, white husky bounded into the room and my heart soared.

He was so cute, how could I not love him?

Petting the thick fur at his neck, I heard my sister's voice as she leaned against the kitchen island.

"What? He's harmless."

"He's a dog, Scar."

Scarlet crossed her arms over her chest and sighed, shaking her head in exasperation.

"You already said yes, Tyler."

I watched him move from the kitchen to where she was standing and as he wrapped his arms around her waist and pulled her close to his chest, her smile widened.

She was happy.

I was happy for her.

But as I watched them have another silent moment, their attention solely on one another, I felt the stirrings of jealousy curl through my stomach. The thought that I would never have what she did – love, affection, a person to come home to every night – was enough to drive me back to the high. But I knew, no matter how much I wanted to, I wouldn't do that.

I needed to try to live again and the drugs weren't going to help me do that. They would thrust me back into the darkness my life had been shrouded in since Spencer's birth and that was a place I couldn't go back to. I *wouldn't* go back to.

I needed to find my light, now.

~

"Tayla?" I was lost in my thoughts as my sister gently pushed my shoulder to gain my attention.

I smiled slightly, hoping she couldn't tell that my mind was anywhere but here. My first Narcotics Anonymous meeting after rehab had me feeling more emotional and vulnerable than I was used to. I'd stood up in front of a bunch of strangers and said my truth.

Hi. My name is Tayla and I'm an addict.

Afterwards, Scarlet wanted to do some food shopping so that was where we were headed. With Tyler home on leave, she hadn't had a chance to do her weekly grocery run, so I offered to go with her.

Reaching over the center console to grasp her hand in mine, I needed her to know how much it meant that she took me to my first meeting. The first of many, I was sure.

"Thank you for coming with me. I know I don't say it enough, but I love you." Her eyes fogged over with emotion and I squeezed her fingers tightly around mine as I felt my own face warming with the need to let my tears fall. Except, this time, they weren't stemming from sadness. They were happy tears, joyful, thankful. I was finding reasons to push through the darkness, reasons to keep fighting and I knew I owed every one of them to her.

She'd believed in me when I couldn't find the strength to, she *never* stopped fighting for me.

Having parked in a spot just outside the store, she turned fully to me, her eyes filled with concern and care; emotions I wasn't sure I deserved, but needed to see from her.

"I know that, I've always known that. Even when I thought I would lose hope of pulling you out of that life, I knew you cared about us and never meant to hurt anyone. If I thought otherwise, I wouldn't have fought so hard. But you came back to us, Tayla. That's all that matters, okay?"

I nodded, felt her reassuring squeeze of my fingers that helped calm my fears of the future and the shame of the many mistakes I made when it came to her. A lesser person wouldn't have stuck with me throughout the past year, when all I'd cared about was myself and my needle, *nothing more*. But Scarlet never gave up on me. I doubted she ever would.

Huffing a sigh, her eyes softened with humor and I found myself smiling again.

"God, we're a couple of saps, huh? Come here."

A tearful laugh left me as she wound her arms around my waist and hugged me tightly, not letting go until our tears had subsided, our mutual sorrow for the moments lost to the shadow of the past falling away, to be replaced with renewed hope and a love only sisters could share.

The loud sound that came from my stomach a

moment later interrupted the moment and I laughed into her shirt, with a disbelieving shake of my head.

"Let's get going so we can get dinner started."

"Yeah." I grinned at her as I got out of the car and snagged a cart from the front of the store.

"Do you have the list, Scar?" I called to my sister, just loudly enough for her to hear me in the next aisle and I heard her lighthearted laughter that followed.

"Who needs a list? I've got Tyler texting me everything we need!"

I took my items from the shelf as I heard her answer, knocking my shoulder gently into hers as I reached her in the bread aisle, where she was perusing the array of bagels on the shelves in front of her.

"Just get the plain ones." Scanning her choices, she shook her head and I grinned, knowingly. A lot of things had changed during our separation of the last year or so, but my sister's indecisive nature was not one of them. She couldn't make a decision to save her life, especially when it came to food.

She wasn't a picky eater, in the least, but that didn't stop her from weighing her options, no matter how small.

"But you like whole wheat."

"So? Get what you want, Scar." I could have laughed at her as her little nose scrunched up tight and her mouth settled in a bemused line, because it wasn't that big a deal.

Moving down the aisle toward the shelf that housed the condiments and various kinds of spices, like ginger, garlic and parsley, I searched for what we'd need. It seemed fitting, since my best-loved food was none other than pasta.

I grabbed a few things I knew we'd need for dinner and spared a look over to my sister, only to witness her taking one bag of each bagel from the tray and dropping them into our cart, her raised eyebrow daring me to say something. Shrugging at her antics, I let it go.

"Is that everything we need?" Tilting her head, she looked down at her iPhone in her hand, where she read off the small list of items we'd come to the market for.

"We still need to get bottled water and juice. Other than that, we're good."

Nodding, we linked arms as we went in search of the juice aisle and I felt my chest warm with a weird sense of awareness. As if someone was watching us. I shook off the thought of it, unwilling to let anything ruin our sister time.

Time I didn't think I'd have with her. Time I almost missed out on, because of my own selfishness and stupid decisions. I was intent on soaking up every minute of it.

"I'll be right back, I left my purse in the car," I said, knowing if I didn't go and retrieve it, she'd wind up paying for my things, too.

She was just too kind, too selfless.

Dropping the large jar of pickles into the front of the cart, Scarlet shook her head, ready to insist on paying. But I was one step ahead of her.

"Tayla, it's fine. I don't want..."

"What?" I called, half-heartedly.

"Tayla, I'm serious..."

Shrugging my shoulders as I quickly backed out of the aisle, I feigned ignorance.

"Sorry, Scar, I can't hear you! Be right back."

Letting out a soft laugh, I rushed toward the exit doors on the side of the building, hoping the car wasn't too far away. God knew, my sister would pay for everything before I came back and I'd be pissed, because she didn't have to. That wouldn't stop her, though.

"Oh!" I mustn't have been paying much attention to where I was going, because the second I stepped out of the automatic doors of the store, I knocked into a large wall of muscle, the chest that collided with mine firm and hard, with rips of a six-pack clearly visible beneath the fabric of the tank top he sported.

Jerk, I thought to myself, a hand to my heart as I waited for my chest to stop quaking with shock. The nerve of this man, to just knock into someone without even looking...

The aggravated train of thought was stopped short when my eyes traveled to the offender's face and my heart seemed to stop altogether.

Asher. I would have recognized those brilliant blue eyes anywhere.

Filled with surprised mischief and hungry heat, his eyes did crazy things to my heart even as I wanted to be unaffected by his charms. I couldn't, though. Because just the way he looked at me knocked me off balance and had me questioning why I was staying away from him in the first place.

I'm going to fuck you, now. His words from last night, filled with lust and hungered devotion, whispered again through my mind and I tried to shake them loose as I straightened my top and dropped my eyes to his feet, hoping he'd let me go, because God knew I couldn't be the one to pull away right then.

Have some mercy, Ash. I'm trying to stay away for your own good.

But, no, he wouldn't make it easy on me, I knew that just from the look in those brilliant eyes of his. He was beautiful and tempting; trouble and safety. Everything I needed and everything I was too afraid to admit I desired. It was a good thing I'd gotten used to avoiding my feelings.

Because being around him again would have broken my resolve.

Moving back a step, I watched his feet shuffle closer, the sneakers he wore the same color as the rest of his outfit, all black. He wore a lot of dark, foreboding colors, I was realizing. It seemed so fitting, since to me, he was the epitome of trouble. It should have re-minded me to steer clear, but it did the complete oppo-site. Instead, I noticed how his eyes gleamed against the contrast of his black shirt and dark washed jeans, his Nike sneakers matching except for the small, white logo placed on the side of his shoes. Even the watch that rested along his thick wrist matched, the gold face reminding me of his eyes; bright, blinding, surprising.

"Look at me, Tayla." The words were spoken with a directness I hadn't heard come from him in our time together, yet they tugged at something primitive in-side of me. The instinct to know why had my face moving toward the sound, my gaze automatically reaching the eyes that had haunted my thoughts all day.

Why did I let him affect me this way? I wondered to myself, knowing that if I asked him the questions racing through my head in that moment, I would un-doubtedly embarrass myself.

It was just sex. But I couldn't stop obsessing over it.

"Tayla." It was just my name. Two syllables. Five letters. I had heard it my entire life, so why, as he spoke the word, was my core clenching in renewed need and my body coming alive with craving for his touch?

It was crazy. Irrelevant. Stupid. I shouldn't be feeling these things, not for him. We'd only just met and I wanted more.

I wanted so much more, but had nothing to truly give him.

Walk away. My mind warned me.

Move closer. My body answered.

Give in. My core ached with heat, an unlit fire only this man could tend to.

And I had only known him a day.

God, I was in trouble.

"What are you so afraid of, Angel?" My breath became ragged as he approached me, his footsteps slow and his eyes hot on mine, never straying, never relenting in their focus.

Isn't this what I'd wanted, all this time? To feel wanted? To feel safe with a man I know won't hurt me?

But he will. It's only a matter of time.

My rational thoughts were a painful reminder that my heart wasn't mine to give away.

It belonged to a little boy that lived miles and miles away, just out of my reach. The second I laid my eyes on him, I fell in love.

And from that moment on, I knew what true, unconditional love meant. It wasn't fancy cars or gifts on every birthday. It wasn't a hug or a nice card for the holidays. It wasn't any of those things.

It was the way my heart seemed to grow as my baby boy lay there, in my arms. It was the dreams I'd had for him for so long, dreams I had no hope of experiencing with him. It was the knowledge that he may never know the love I felt for him, then and now.

It was the pain in my chest, the turning knife within my gut as I let him go, forever. My heart belonged with him and, because of the choice I made that day, it would never be truly whole again.

I didn't realize how close Asher was until my shoulders pressed into the wall behind me, the rough texture of the brick of the building bringing me back to the here and now, with Asher's large, hard, beautiful body surrounding mine, as if that would protect me from the pain of the world around us.

The emotion in his eyes drew me in as he caged me to his body, the wall behind me blocking me from the escape—route my heart screamed for me to find.

"Answer the fuckin' question, baby."

"I... I don't know." The hoarse sound of his laughter pressed into my skin at my cheek and the warmth of his breath along my overheated skin caused goosebumps to spread at the contact.

He was too close, he smelled too damn good...

Oh God, I couldn't do this.

"I would never hurt you, Angel. Can't you see that? *Feel* that?" His voice was barely above a whisper and though I heard – no, *felt* – the raw, real honesty in his words, I couldn't let myself believe it. My heart wanted to, God, did it want to. My head? That was a different story.

The last time I truly trusted someone, they

wrecked me. Made me believe I was broken, only good enough to pass around to his friends whenever the mood struck him. And the sad part was, I'd believed those lies he told me.

Because my self worth had been shattered under his cruelty, his whispered comments and misplaced jealousy. Trusting Trent had just been the first in an avalanche of God—awful mistakes, one after another, until I couldn't see a way out of the wreckage of my life. I had a second chance now. But that didn't mean I was ready to risk everything again.

I was clean, now. If Asher hurt me, whether it was on purpose or by accident, it didn't much matter. My heart was barely whole and the thought of having it torn to pieces again was terrifying.

I couldn't live through that again. I just... couldn't.

"Asher, I can't do this. Last night was fun, but that's all it was."

"Bullshit." The word was growled out between his clenched teeth and looking up, up, up at him, I found he looked twice as big when he was angry. A few minutes ago, I would have told you that Asher was good, sweet, rough around the edges but soft on the inside. Now, I wasn't so sure.

Right then, he looked livid and it was me he was upset with.

I gasped for breath as he pressed me back against the brick wall behind me, his narrowed eyes on me the entire time – holding me captive. His mouth was set in a firm line, as if he was made of the hardest stone.

I cowered on the inside, though I knew at the heart of me that he would never lay a hand on me, never hurt me like that. He shook his head once and, biting my lip, I tried to stop myself from trembling as the heat of his chest pressed against my body, making me relive the heat and intensity of last night.

"Last night was everything. You know it. I know it. You can lie to yourself if you want, but it won't change the truth, baby. You were *made* for me."

"No," I gasped out, wanting him to take those words back as their truth hung in the air between us.

"Yes." As he dropped his head to press his face against my cheek, I felt firm fingers wrap around my hips, his knee parting my legs as he held me there, having no intention of letting me go anytime soon.

"It wasn't... I'm not..." I stuttered out a sad excuse of a rebuttal and, grinning, Asher bent his head until our lips were merely an inch apart, reminding me of how he'd made me feel last night, the way he touched and kissed me as if I was the only woman he wanted... needed.

"Tell me you don't want me, Tayla."

"W—what?" Pulling back an inch, he raised his thick eyebrows in challenge, as if he knew I wouldn't be able to lie to him, not about this.

"Tell me you don't want this between us and I'll go. But don't you dare lie, baby. Because you and me? We're inevitable. You can't deny that."

Oh, but I could. I couldn't risk giving my heart to a man again. Even Asher, as much as I wished I could. So, I lied.

It was, unfortunately, a talent I had perfected after years of lying in order to get by, feeding my addiction time and time again, even when it came at the cost of my family's love and trust.

"I... I don't *want* you, Asher. I never did."

Fight or flight.

Sparks licked up my spine as the itch to run heaved my heart. I didn't dare look at the man above me, his hold on me now tight with anguish instead of the gentle way he'd held onto me mere seconds before. Pressing my hands against his chest, I pushed him away for what I knew would be the last time.

There was no coming back from this.

Run, my mind screamed, knowing that if I didn't, I would break down and let him in – let him see how desperately I wanted him, needed him, right then.

Turning away from him, I ran away, like the coward I'd come to be.

I was just picking up after dinner when I felt a ding in my back pocket. My heart sped up in the hopes it was Asher, but I knew, by the way I'd run away from him like some frightened little girl, that was a very low possibility.

It wasn't that I was afraid of him. I was afraid that being with him would be a mistake. I was afraid of getting my heart broken again. Why did he even want me?

It didn't make any sense.

Piling the dishes into the washer and starting the cycle, I took the time to wipe my hands dry with an oven towel before ascending the stairs that would take me to my room.

I needed a bath and bubbles and a good book.

And then I needed to figure out how to get Asher out of my head, for good.

Ever since leaving this morning, I'd thought of him and the way he'd touched me, kissed me, like there were no one else in this world he'd rather touch, rather kiss.

And silly me for believing it.

He'd told me himself that he wasn't a good man. But that, I didn't believe, not after the way he'd taken care of me last night.

He was a good friend, a good brother, from what I could see. He'd taken a chance on my brother and his music when no one else had.

And he'd made me feel safer and more cherished than ever before.

He'd make a great boyfriend to some lucky girl out there. One with a full heart and lively spirit to offer him. It just wouldn't be me. I was too broken, too damaged.

He was better off without me.

"You okay?" God, I wished people would stop asking me that damn question.

Turning around, I smiled to find Tyler standing in the hall. He was shrugging his jacket on as he looked at me with concern, waiting on my sister, most likely.

"I think I made a mistake, Ty." Dropping my head, I fiddled with the end of my shirt, wishing I knew what the right thing to do was. I knew Asher would be good to me. I knew that he wouldn't treat me like Trent had, like a piece of meat to pass around. A tremor slid down my back at the thought of reliving that dark, twisted time in my life. If I never had to hear from that man again, it would be just fine with me.

Sleeping with Asher had felt good at the time. Right. Like being right there, with him, in his arms, was exactly where I was meant to be. But a thought like that could be dangerous to me. Hoping for something with him was foolish, especially with the life I'd lived over the past few years. At one time, I was a good girl, solely focused on getting good grades and helping mom in the shop whenever I could. And then I'd met Trent and everything, all the things I'd hoped for and strived for, weren't important anymore.

Love was like a riptide washing into the shore, breaking through all of my carefully thought out plans, my dreams for the future and what I could someday be. Once the tide rolled in, there was nothing of the girl I once was left in its wake.

I didn't know how far I'd fallen until it was too late. Until I was on the streets, every night, begging for scraps, for anything to take the pain away.

Before Spencer came along, drugs were like chocolate to me. The occasional craving, when I saw everyone else indulging in it. It wasn't until I felt the true and incredibly strong pain of letting go of my baby that I let my cravings take hold of me. That itch just beneath my skin became everything, controlled *everything*. Morning to night, it was all I wanted, all I needed to feel numb to the torture of knowing my baby was out there, being loved but not by me.

I didn't care about anything after he came along, because the one thing I'd gotten right in my life had been taken from me.

No, even worse; it hadn't been taken from me, I just gave it away.

"How do you know it was a mistake?" Hearing Ty's footsteps behind me, I begrudgingly turned around, knowing he had no idea how far I had fallen. I doubted my sister had told him much of anything, just that I'd gone to rehab and the reason why. She was always protecting me, even when I failed her, time and again. I had no idea how she hadn't given up on me after the way I treated her and the family I had left.

"What's his name?" Looking up at Tyler, I frowned, unsure how he knew I'd been referring to a man. He was one, so maybe he could see things clearer than I did.

"Asher." Squeezing my shoulder, he pulled me into his chest, rubbed my back with a brotherly hand, a silent gesture that I could talk to him. He wouldn't judge me, or my choices.

I knew that much from the way he treated my sister as if she was made of glass, always putting her needs before his own.

So, I told him. About Trent. About the drugs. About Spencer, and inevitably about Asher. How he made me feel, how he soothed my darkness, how he chased away the pain in my heart. In many ways, our night together had given me much more than I'd offered up to him. And the worst part? Asher didn't even know it.

The moment I finished my story, I could feel a change – something lightening my heart, loosening the heavy weight of guilt and regret I carried with me for all the mistakes I made in my past. Just saying them out loud gave a voice to them and it helped. Maybe not completely, but I still felt the relief of it.

"Don't close your heart off to something that could heal you from the pain of your past, Tay. Trust me, I was so closed off, it took weeks of pestering me for a scrap of attention for your sister to even get a glimpse of what was in my heart. I pushed her away because I wasn't sure I deserved her. Maybe Asher isn't your forever, but you'll never know if you don't give him a chance."

Turning into his open arms, I let myself believe what he was saying. Believe that love wasn't lost for me. That maybe, someday, it wouldn't be this hard to let someone in.

Too bad the one person who'd been willing to knock down my walls was the very person I'd pushed away for good.

12

TAYLA

THREE WEEKS LATER

My head stung as I peeled my eyes open a sliver, the blindingly bright sunlight coming in from my bedroom blinds having woken me up way too early for my liking.

"Good morning, sunshine!" my sister all but sang from the side of my bed and, frowning, I rolled over and buried my face as far into the pillows as I could.

It was a Saturday morning and I didn't have my meeting until noon. Having spent half the night up, tossing and turning with dreams of my sweet little boy in my head, all I wanted to do was fall back into a hopefully deep, dreamless sleep.

"I have a surprise for you." Peeking up at her with one eye, I wasn't sure whether I believed her.

When we were kids, she would pull me out of bed early, just to bother me. She was annoying, but hell, I was sure I was, too.

"Scar, I don't want to go in with you."

Going in to work with her wasn't my idea of a good day.

"I have today off. I thought we could go shopping before your meeting."

Sitting up in bed, I realized I hadn't gone shopping in I—didn't—know—how—long. Last week I'd started working at the flower shop, again opening the store for my mom so she could sleep in on the weekends. And during the week, I mainly just helped during busy times. I had just been saving my checks, not needing to spend as I was staying with my parents until I could figure out what I wanted to do about a place of my own.

Maybe getting some cute clothes would help me feel like *me* again.

I wanted to be *me* again. I wanted to find the things that made me feel alive, made me happy, even if just for a few hours.

I didn't want to feel empty anymore.

I needed to be *me*, again.

13

TAYLA

"*T*his is Asher's studio." I said dumbly, as Scarlet pulled her car up to the curb right in front of a tall, brick building with large, scrawled writing across the front of it. It was a worn place, one that wasn't shiny and new like many of the other businesses closer to town, but this one it had a certain *charm* to it. An old, rustic feel to it.

"I know." Pulling her keys from the ignition, she got out of the car and confused, I followed her lead.

The idea of seeing *my* Asher again had my chest squeezing with regret and excitement and though I was sure he didn't want to see me after what I'd said, I wanted the chance to lay my eyes on him, again.

A long, stone path led to double glass doors with brass handles. I followed Scarlet inside, unsure of where I was going or why we were even here. After my meeting, I'd thought we were going shopping at the mall across town, but instead she'd brought me here. Shortly after my night with Asher, I confided in her about our night together, about how I'd pushed him away out of fear of getting hurt. Scarlet understood because, just like me, she'd been hurt by a man before.

Trusting the wrong man had her reeling from the pain of it just like I'd been. I wasn't surprised when she told me she thought I was making a mistake, letting a man like him go. Especially after Blake told us that Asher *knew*.

Asher *knew* I was an addict, fresh out of rehab for the third time and he'd still wanted me. Still wanted more.

Letting my eyes drift to the polished wood floors in the entryway, I couldn't help be impressed by the place. Asher wasn't just a musician. He owned a business, a recording studio that artists all over Dallas relied on to hone their voice, their sound.

My hand glided over the long, mahogany bannister as I imagined Asher bending me over it, his callused fingers wrapping around my hips from behind as he squeezed my ass in his hands in need for me, as if he couldn't stay away for one more *second*.

God. I needed to get a grip. It had been weeks since I'd set my eyes on him, or even heard a word from him.

But I couldn't blame him, could I? I hadn't just turned him away. I hadn't just told him I wasn't in a place for love right now. I pushed him away, been cold and unfeeling, as if he meant nothing... *as if we meant nothing.*

I don't want you, Asher. I never did. My parting words to him whispered in my mind.

God, I was heartless. A liar. A coward. The man scared me, made me want to shield myself from the heartbreak he would bring. Closing my eyes, I saw him standing there in the grocery store, his big, burly arms crossed over his chest, his tattoos peeking out from underneath his a—little—too—tight t-shirt.

God, I wanted him. *Desperately.*

But that didn't mean it was a good idea.

Looking over at Scarlet as we sat in the lobby, I knew the smirk painted across her face oh—so—well.

That's why she'd brought me here. To push me to talk to him sooner.

I knew she meant well, but right then I wanted to throttle her.

"Tayla, it's time you took back your life. *Talk* to him. You know he's been asking about you to Blake. He may be hurt that you rejected him, but he isn't *blind,* sis."

What if he turned me away? The fear of that possibility had me realizing that no matter how much time passed, I would still want him.

Bite the bullet. I told myself. It was worth the risk of getting hurt, just to see him, again.

Getting up from my chair, I pulled out my phone to text him, but before I could unlock it, heavy footsteps approached from behind me and a gruff voice I would recognize anywhere stopped me in my tracks.

"What the hell are *you* doing here?" He didn't just sound annoyed that I was here, he was *mad.* And for the first time, it was completely directed towards me.

14

ASHER

"*Tayla*." I'd heard her voice from a fucking mile away or at least it felt like it. I was in my office, nursing the hangover to end all hangovers, when heels clacked on the floors above me and I just knew. My angel was here.

Except, she wasn't mine. I'd spent all night drinking my sorrows away, remembering the moment she uttered the words I never knew could hurt *so much*.

I don't want you.

I made her say them, but once she had, I knew she meant them. The first girl to ever get under my damn skin was rejecting me, casting me aside before I'd even had the chance to take her on a real, proper date. And I wanted to.

Girls were always a given to me. They were always around me, vying for my attention from the first time I set my sights on one in junior high. I'd never had to work in order to get a woman's attention. Never even tried to do all of the extra things a girl might want from a man. No, the easy way was always my way. I was a lazy, arrogant bastard and I knew it.

Tayla, she made me want the chase. To earn her trust and her love. I wanted it all. Every—fucking—thing. But only if it was with her.

Too bad she didn't want me. Didn't even want to try.

Never knew a girl I barely even knew could cut that deep. But she had.

Getting up from my desk, I resolved to push her out of my life, for good. If she didn't want me, fine. But she didn't get to show up at my business, for God knows what reason. Maybe she needed a job. Maybe she could sing.

Maybe she liked my brother better. As that thought made its way into my head, I stormed down the stairs so fast I was sure I'd break them and ploughed into the door that led to the first floor, intent on finding my angel and banishing her for good.

My sanity relied on it. My chest stung with the pain of rejection as soon as I laid eyes on her as she sat in my lobby in a little sundress, her hair up in a messy bun with a few strands falling around her pretty face. *God*, would I ever stop wanting her, craving her like this?

I wanted to look away, order her to leave and never come back.

I couldn't look away, though. I was a starving man, looking at my last meal. That's what she did to me. I couldn't stop if I'd tried. And trust me when I say I had. *Tried*. All night long, every night for the past three weeks, begging for answers at the bottom of each drink I took, every beer I emptied.

My answers all ended with her. It was like a sick joke.

If I couldn't get her out of my heart, I had to get

her out of my life. Just a look from a few feet away and I was desperate for scraps, needing just *one more taste.*

Fuck. I couldn't do it, anymore.

"What the *hell* are you doing here?" My voice wasn't mine, anymore. It was a roar, a growl from deep, deep in my chest where the lingering pain of her dismissal of me lay dormant. I sounded like a caveman, demanding dinner from his woman. A bear, growling to the heavens in the dead of night. I knew I would scare her away for good if I wasn't careful. But right then, I just didn't care.

I would have given her the world if she'd let me. Instead, she'd pushed me away, shunned me as if what we had meant *nothing.*

Hell, maybe she was right. Maybe this was a Big. Fucking. Mistake.

"A—asher..." Her usually strong, sweet voice cracked and stuttered and I wished it didn't bother me that I was scaring her this way.

But it did. *My angel.*

Looking down at her feet, she was that shy girl all over again, needing my touch to make her feel beautiful, *worthy.*

Turning her head so our eyes met, I saw her cheeks flush red. No doubt remembering our night together, I mused.

"I—I wanted to see you, Asher."

Well, I hadn't been expecting that, had I?

"My office is down here, *Angel.*" I said with a sigh, knowing I couldn't turn her away, no matter how much I wanted to for my own damn sanity.

"This is your office?" Her pretty face tilted up to meet my stare and, nodding, I opened the door for her, wanting to watch that little ass of hers as she walked inside. She may have crushed me something fierce, but I still wanted her like the air I fucking breathed.

She wasn't just a passing interest to me.

She. Was. Fucking. It.

Mine.

"After you." I caught a whiff of her sweet cherry scent as she passed me and had to swallow the groan on my lips.

God, she smelled good.

"Asher, I..." Closing the door behind me, I made myself look at her even though I knew I shouldn't. Looking at her was painful now. Even being around her hurt knowing how she felt.

I don't want you, Asher. I never did.

Looking over at her, I noticed her face wasn't the mask of indifference I'd seen before. Her big, hazel eyes were staring up at me, sadness and longing evident in her gaze. Her mouth was turned down in a sad, little smile and the sight of it had me wanting to pull her into my arms and kiss her until that pitiful look disappeared for good. She *had* wanted me. I wasn't imagining that, I realized.

Why? Why had she lied to me?

She looked down as I took a step closer, needing to be closer, closer, closer to her. I could take that sadness away from her. I could make her happy. I knew I could. If only she'd let me.

I knew she was used to doing things on her own, suffering in silence. I couldn't take her painful past away from her, but I could give her a reason to smile. Every day. A million reasons.

If I had any say in it, she'd never be alone, again.

"Please, Ash, say something."

"You lied, didn't you?" Her eyes came back to mine at that, the longing I'd seen before replaced by warmth, hope even.

"It's easier..." She stumbled over her words as she peered up at me, our bodies only a mere foot away, now.

"Easier for who?" My hands caught her little waist, pulling her in as close as I could, so she couldn't get away from my questions, guessing she would shy away, or lie, again.

She'd put her walls up, protecting herself at all costs and now I had to knock them down, *for good*. Because she didn't need them with me.

I may have been a player in the past, but now? I was a one-woman man.

And it was her.

"It's not gonna be easy, baby. I fuckin' want you. I've tried to stop, I've tried drinking you out of my head. But it doesn't work. How could it? You're under my skin. Right *here*." Grasping her hand in mine, I placed it on my chest, right over my heart so she could feel how gone over her I was.

One night with her and that's all it took. She closed her eyes as I pulled her impossibly closer, lowering my head until our mouths were a breath apart, her sweet breath on my lips, my fingers roaming hungrily to her ample ass.

"Tell me you don't want me, baby. *Lie*," I dared her. Her pretty eyes looked up at me, wide and warm and beautiful and I knew she couldn't do it... she couldn't deny it.

"Please, Ash." She wanted an out. A way to avoid the pull between us. But I just shook my head, approaching her slowly, caging her in until the backs of her knees met my desk and once I had her, I smiled wide, knowing she couldn't get away so easily, now.

"You said you didn't want me, but Angel, I don't believe it. Not for a second. This..." rubbing my thumb over the apple of her cheek, I watched the blush blossom beneath my hand, just another sign that I affected her just as much as she affected me, "... this tells me all I need to know."

"Asher." Her fingers pressed against the collar of my shirt as she pled my name and, looking down at them, I was sure she was getting ready to push me away. But then she just looked up at me and I knew she felt it, too. She felt what we could be, if only she would give it a chance.

Curling her nails into my shirt, she sighed in surrender and it was all I needed. My heart was in my throat as I moved my hands to her hips and hoisted her up to the edge of my desk, settling myself between her parted thighs and tilting her chin up to mine, eager for the taste that I knew she'd give me.

"Asher..." Her voice was little more than a whisper as she said my name and I moved closer, my lips barely an inch from hers now.

"I'm *sorry*, Ash. I'm sorry for pushing you away. This..." I fucking *shook* with need as she pulled my face into her hands in the gentlest touch I'd ever fucking felt and I knew, just knew, she got it, now. Got the fact that we weren't just a temporary thing... we weren't a mistake, a one night stand to be easily forgotten once morning came.

No, we were *more*.

"This is real," she continued, in that same

breathy, sexy—as—fuck whisper, "and I'm scared, but I want it. I really want it, Ash."

"Fuck, Tayla." It was all I could get out before she pushed forward, slanting her warm, wet lips over mine and almost instantly licked against them, begging for more than just the taste I'd hoped for.

She was going to be the death of me.

"There's plenty of time for kissing. Like tonight." Looking up from her lap, she beamed a smile at me that made my heart stop altogether.

I was in trouble if just her smile got to me.

"Like, a date?" She sounded so hopeful, so happy and it was just what I wanted for her. I didn't want to see the sad, troubled girl anymore.

I wanted to see her happy.

"Yeah. But I want to see you in a dress. Think you can do that for me?" Smiling from ear to ear, she nodded.

"I think so."

15

TAYLA

*P*ulling at the ends of my dress, I tried not to overthink everything as I swayed on the porch swing in front of my parents house. It was a habit I'd picked up as a little girl. If I let my mind wander, I would torture myself with a million 'what ifs', a thousand reasons why I shouldn't take risks or go for things I really wanted. Asher was one of those things.

The man had the biggest heart and from the second I met him, I'd felt safe with him. Like he would protect me, at all costs. I wasn't sure where that feeling had come from, but I trusted in it. *Trusted in him.*

Given my history with men, I didn't think it was a good idea to start something new, so soon. I'd only been sober all of three months and still attended NA meetings twice a week. I had a mountain of emotional baggage to sort through and heal from and it would take a lot of work to do so. I was used to working through those things alone. I was used to relying on myself and *only* myself.

It was easier that way. Pushing Asher away was

my way of protecting myself, because loving him had the power to break me, *completely*.

If I let him in and my darkness scared him away, I wasn't sure I would come back from that. It hurt to do it, but I thought I was doing the right thing, sparing us both from pain and the inevitable end of things when he either got bored with me or realized I wasn't worth the trouble that being with me would bring. I would *always* be in recovery. I would *always* be an addict. It didn't matter if I lived to be a hundred, that dark part of me that craved the high would always lie dormant, deep inside of me.

There was *always* going to be the temptation, the risk that I would be weak and relapse. I wanted to say that I was strong enough to stay clean for the long haul, but that felt damn near impossible some days. Some days I felt weak and only the support of my family stopped me from using again. I would always need drugs as a crutch. I may never be able to rid myself of that darkness drugs caused in my life.

Was that something Asher could live with?

"God, you're fucking beautiful." His deep voice reached inside of me, touching all the dark places within my fractured heart. Looking up at him, I saw him leaning against the railing, his ocean blue eyes settled right on me.

I felt that hot stare right down to my core. Squeezing my legs together, I smiled shyly, not wanting him to see how he affected me. Physically, emotionally and, if the wetness between my thighs was any indication, *sexually*.

"Ready to go?" Nodding, I got up from the swing and took his hand, following him to his truck, sweet anticipation filling my chest at the prospect of spending the night with this man.

~

"Where are you taking me?"

"It's a surprise. You'll like it." Asher clasped a hand over my knee as he pulled the car over to park. His hand gripped the wheel loosely, though the way his long, tanned fingers wrapped around it told me he had full control and concentration, even as he used his other hand to stroke the tingling skin of my knee. My mind wandered, wondering if he would use that kind of tightly held control and in bed tonight and my pussy ached at just the thought of it; arousal spreading between my thighs instantly.

"Come on, dirty girl. We're here." *Busted.* Feeling the deep blush covering my face, I knew he saw just where my thoughts had gone.

"You like it." I teased, wanting to get under his skin just like he'd slipped under mine. Shaking his head at me, Asher pulled me from my seat and closed the door behind me with a bemused smile.

Looking up, up, up at him as he led me away, I realized I'd been wrong about him. He wasn't a bad boy. He wasn't a ladies man. Maybe in his past he'd been that man but looking at him, now, I realized he had enough love in that heart of his to slay my demons if I gave him the chance.

Everything about him made me feel safe and I was pretty sure that it would be easy to fall if he would be the one catching me.

"Hey, look at me." His deep, concern-filled voice pulled me from my thoughts and I looked up at him, instantly feeling warmth spread through me just at the way he looked at me. A big, imposing man like him should have scared me, intimidated me, at least. But not him.

He made me feel... everything.

"Sorry, I'm good, Ash. Promise." Squeezing my waist, Asher pulled me into his chest and nodded, relieved at my answer.

"Come on, I think you'll like this."

Taking his hand, I followed him inside a tall building to an elevator with a sign above it. It read: *Welcome to Adventure land.* My chest tightened with heady excitement, knowing exactly where we were.

"Adventure land?" I'd *loved* this place as a kid. I was pretty sure he'd gotten that tidbit of information from Blake and that just made this surprise even sweeter.

Gnawing at my lip, I wondered what he had in store. I hadn't been here since I was young. My dad would take Scarlet, Blake and I for the day, make us go on all the kiddy rides before braving the roller coasters we'd been barely tall enough to ride. It was like being a kid, again.

"I'm going to want to do everything, you know. You'll get bored just waiting around, won't you?"

"I could never get bored with you, baby. Come on." Tugging me gently into his side, he pulled me into the elevator and I couldn't help the smile that stayed on my face the whole way up.

16

ASHER

*W*atching her was becoming my new favorite pastime. The way her long, blonde hair flowed down her back as she walked past the food carts lining the entrance to the park had my fingers itching to run through it and feel its softness. The minute we stepped inside the gates, her eyes lit up like Christmas fucking morning. It was beautiful to watch.

I'd learned from Scarlet that her favorite thing to do as a little girl was to come here for summer weekends. Her dad would take a day off from work and bring the whole family down here for a day filled with cotton candy, popcorn and kiddy rides. I'd wanted to do something for her, something to put a smile on her face. Judging by the way she hadn't stopped smiling since we got here, I had got it right.

This woman had been through more than anyone should have to. She'd been alone for far too fucking long, with no one to turn to when life got her down. That was changing, from here on out. I was here, now. I could look after her, protect her from her demons and the harshness of the world. I could be that for her. I wouldn't let her down, I vowed.

Gripping her hand firmly, I pulled her in close, unwilling to let her get too far as we walked through the crowd of people around us. My hands sunk into the dewy softness of her hair, my head dipping toward hers as my chest swelled with the need for a taste of her.

I could never get enough of her taste. Her mouth came up to mine easily, the smile on her face fading as her eyes filled with lust, a heat causing my jeans to tighten as I grew hard for her, right there, in the middle of a damn amusement park, of all places. A groan crawled up my throat as I kissed her hard, letting her feel the hunger I felt for her whenever she was near. Her little tongue flicked against mine and my balls ached, fucking ached with my need for her. *Now.*

We should get out of here. The thought came to my mind in an instant and though I was tempted, I knew she would want to stay and ride at least a few roller coasters, maybe have some cotton candy before the night was out.

Pulling away from her now—swollen lips, I begrudgingly released her, the little minx.

"What do you want to do first?"

"Everything."

"Lead the way, then."

17

TAYLA

I was pretty sure the smile hadn't left my face all night long. After we'd seen every attraction and ridden every ride, I let Asher lead me away and towards the exits, knowing that a fun night like tonight was just what I'd needed. I needed the reminder that there were still simple, easy pleasures in life. Like amusement parks and cotton candy. Fast rides and stolen kisses when I least expected them. The feeling that I really was okay, I was safe.

The feeling of Asher's callused thumb rubbing over my palm was slowly lulling me to sleep. We were at his house, having decided to watch a movie and order pizza, since all we'd eaten all night was cotton candy and an *amazing* fried dough. I couldn't help hoping I would fall asleep, right here, in his arms. I wanted to spend the night with him. I just wanted to be *near* him.

It wasn't about sex with him. Though that was earth—shattering between us, what really drew me to the big, kind man beside me wasn't his muscles or tattoos, or how absolutely beautiful – no, gorgeous – he was. No, it was his heart. The way he was honest, down to his bones.

I hadn't had a very good track record with men. I'd been with a man who used me, disregarded me when I wasn't his priority. And when that hadn't been enough, he got me pregnant and then ran for the hills.

Let's just say he hadn't been a keeper.

My ex would always be a source of pain and regret for me, but I found myself feeling lucky that he'd come into my life. Because if he hadn't, would I be sitting here, with Asher?

I doubted it.

"What are you thinking so hard about, Angel?" I felt warm, firm fingers grasp my chin and turn my head until my eyes landed on his piercing sky-blue ones and something inside of me settled, calmed. It didn't matter what Trent had done, though I would never forget it. Trent was the past. Asher was my now. I didn't know where we'd go from here, but right now, he was here with me.

Pressing myself into his side, I looked up into his eyes and saw the warmth there and knew this was the moment I would let him in. He would wait for me, I knew that.

But for some reason, I knew I could trust him. I could put my faith in him.

I knew it down to every bone in my body.

"Can I stay?" His hold on me tightened as my question resonated and a relieved grin spread his lips. He was expecting me to push him away, make him work for it.

But I wanted this. I wanted to hope that happiness was possible for me again. I had a feeling Asher was a big part of that happiness.

"Come here." He didn't just say the words, he growled them.

I melted inside, my core tightening with arousal for a repeat of our night together, my heart pounding with anticipation and longing that only he could cause. My mouth met his softly and the kiss he laid on me was unhurried, much gentler than our others, but I loved it just the same.

I couldn't walk away from him now if I tried. He'd found a way to sliver into my cold, broken heart and there was no getting him out. We were connected; our lips pressing and searching and learning one another's as if it was our first kiss. In a way, it was.

This was our first kiss without my running away, or his begging me to stay. This was our chance to see what we could be, where we could go, together. The fear of what that could mean was at the front of my mind, telling me to be cautious, go slow. But I couldn't stop this, could I?

It was time I stopped trying.

"Upstairs," I whispered against his urgent kisses and, feeling him smile against my lips, I pulled away, taking the time to look up into his smiling eyes. The hunger I saw there left no question as to what he wanted, right then.

"Are you sure, Angel?"

"*Yes.*" The word was just a whisper, an affirmation, a plea, even. But Asher heard it. And he didn't need me to say it twice.

Strong, possessive hands took hold of my waist, lifting me up, up, up until my knees locked around his hips, my dress hiking up high on my thighs as he moved us toward the stairs with ease. He carried me like I weighed nothing and my heart sped in my chest, the feeling of being held like this causing my arousal to build and grow.

"So." His beard scraped against my throat as his mouth left hot, wet kisses along my neck. My thighs squeezed around him, the knowledge that he would be inside me in a matter of minutes making me hot, all over.

"Fucking." His mouth came to mine, then, his tongue teasing mine in long, slow licks that made me melt, right there in his arms.

"Good."

He pulled back as he mounted the last step, stopping in front of his bedroom door. Eyes dark with desire had a sense of need filling my chest in a heady buzz of arousal.

Reaching for the door knob, I twisted it open all the while never taking my gaze away from his. Looking away from his hot stare was impossible, I realized. The attraction between us was tangible, now.

Asher set me down on my feet once we were inside, but his hot, lingering stare never left me. *I didn't want it to.*

Instead, he intently held my stare, as if he couldn't look away for even a second. That kind of intensity should have scared me. Looking up into those ocean eyes of his, I realized nothing involving this man scared me.

I hadn't had many good men in my life but I knew, without a doubt, Asher was the best. *And I didn't deserve him.*

"You overthinking' again?" Asher's words were spoken against my ear as his hands moved to the hem of my dress, his fingers dipping below the soft material to explore my bare skin.

"I don't overthink." Despite my instant denial of his softly spoken comment, I knew he was right. It was something I'd done all my life, constantly wondering, worrying about all the 'what ifs', the worst-case scenarios my mind seemed to always think of.

I watched as he dropped his head back and laughed, a loud, warm sound I wanted to hear, again. Again, and again and again.

"Yeah, you do, Angel. You get this look in your eyes and get that little frown..." Clapping a hand over his smirking mouth, I shook my head at his annoyingly handsome face, wondering how he could know me so well, in such a short amount of time.

"Shut up." Grinning more widely, he just looked at me with that look, one of playfulness, of warmth. Moving my hand off his mouth, I didn't give him a chance to get another teasing comment. I just raised my mouth to his and curled my fingers into the collar of his shirt, smiling against the kiss when he grabbed me around my waist again, our need for each other taking over.

"Take your dress off. Now." Hot, heavy heat pooled between my legs as his eyes roved over me, leaving no part of me without that look – hungry, needful, with so much desire I could feel it in my bones. Biting my lip, I felt shy all of a sudden, wondering if he noticed the stretch marks and baby fat that still remained after my pregnancy.

"Stop that." His warm palms came around each side of my face, his eyes on mine, his attention all on me. "You're beautiful, baby. Perfect. Don't ever feel shy with me. You have *nothing* to be ashamed about."

His words were spoken with conviction. *He meant them.* I knew that inherently. Nodding, I reached for the straps of my sundress, letting my fingers slip beneath them, my dress falling off my shoulders and to my feet in a matter of seconds. Closing my eyes, I felt the heat of his stare on me and felt so desired, I wanted to cry.

"Look at me, Tay." My eyes came up to his quickly and my cheeks blushed at the animalistic, hungry way he looked at me – fucking me with his eyes, his lips, as he slowly licked them.

God. If he didn't touch me soon, I was going to jump him.

"On the bed. I want those pretty eyes on me while I take you."

The backs of my knees hit the bed as he told me how he wanted me and my pussy clenched with desire, a hot need unfurling in my belly that I knew wouldn't be sated until he was inside me, again.

Nodding my head frantically, I toed-off my sandals, laying my head back on his pillows as my heart raced with anticipation of what was to come.

Asher gave me a crooked smile as he pulled his shirt over his head, not bothering with the buttons. We were both teetering on the edge, needing one another to anchor us both and calm this storm of desire and pent-up need that brewed between us.

"Jesus. These legs, baby." I had barely a second to appreciate the sight of his bare chest, those glistening abs shining in the dim light of the bedroom. Before I knew what he was doing, he had his head between my legs, kissing his way up, up my thighs and to the place that needed him the most. My mouth dropped open as the hot, wet heat of his mouth moved over my pussy lips, his tongue tracing my entrance as if asking for permission.

God. Lick me there.

"Ash." I moaned out his name, my hands gripping onto his hair with urgency, my body singing with the sensations his mouth was bringing me. This man knew what he was doing, of that I had no doubt.

"Yeah?" he said, pulling his head back and I wanted to yank him right back but just stopped myself.

He knew what he was doing. He was *teasing* me!

"Lick me." It was a plea. A begging whimper. But he just looked up at me with that cocky smirk on his face, obviously in no rush at all.

"Ask me nicely."

"Ash, I need it." Tightening my fingers in his hair, I squirmed beneath him as the tingling ache between my legs began to fade.

"You need what?" His mouth began to slide over my skin again and, shaking beneath him, I sighed in relief and arousal, knowing he was giving in. He was going to give me what my body needed more than my next breath.

His hands. His mouth. His teeth grazing my feverish, tingling skin. His mouth kissing and rubbing over me, leaving no part of me untouched.

"I need you. I need you to *take* me." He didn't know how true those words were, I mused.

"Good girl." And then his tongue was teasing, licking my folds ardently, the heat between us settling into the apex of my thighs. Grabbing at him with seeking fingers on the back of his head, I pulled him deeper into me as my legs went to jelly beneath his ministrations.

"It's perfect, Angel. Every fuckin' time." He groaned out the words, his voice more of a growl as he sank his thickness right in the center of me, spearing me and taking me and *owning* me, as if this was our last chance to feel the powerful pleasure that ignited between us, between these sheets, in this bed.

Any bed, really. Moaning and whimpering and sobbing with a desire I'd never felt before, I came for him, over and over, like a freight train without a brake. His guttural uttering of my name as he creamed inside the condom he'd sheathed himself with was like a prayer, a plea for this to never end, never stop.

"You were *made* for me, Tayla."

"Yes," I moaned out, knowing he was right, *this* was so, so right.

Closing my eyes, I shook with the aftershocks of our lovemaking and sent up a silent prayer that it wouldn't be the last time I felt him inside me, because I knew that, come morning, we'd have to talk about why I had been so adamant in pushing him away, before.

He deserved the truth. He deserved to know why I doubted again and again that he could bear the weight of my demons, the shadows that still followed me into my dreams every night.

Strong, harboring arms wrapped around me and, as I pressed my face to his hard chest, I hoped for a dreamless sleep, just this once.

~

The first thing I noticed when I awoke from a deep, peaceful sleep was that my heart wasn't galloping in my chest, my palms and back weren't drenched with sweat and my head was clear from the surge of panic and confusion I often awoke to after a nightmare took my mind's peace away. It wasn't every night that they took hold of me, but since leaving rehab, they'd come more often. Maybe it was because I didn't have the help of the drugs or my precious high I'd become accustomed to. Dr. Sloan had given me some sleeping pills to help with them, but I barely remembered to take them.

I didn't *want* to have to rely on drugs again. Prescription or not, it still didn't feel right. I was finally sober and sane and *happy*. Looking over to Asher's side of the bed, I knew he had a huge part in that. He didn't make me feel like I had to pretend with him. I could just be myself and he wanted me.

It was hard to let myself trust in that, but I was going to try. For him. For... *this*.

Climbing slowly out of bed, I sat on the edge, wondering what he would want for breakfast. Deciding to see what he had in his fridge and go from there, I found my clothes from the night before on the floor and my purse hanging on his desk chair. Slipping out of the room, I left the door open just enough, not wanting to wake him by closing it.

When was the last time I thought about someone else's needs before my own? I hadn't needed to in a long time. Looking back at him curled up on the bed, his head resting on a pillow and his long, lean legs tangled up in the blankets, I realized I wanted to, with him.

I wanted to take care of him just as he'd cared for me. I wanted to be what he needed, a safe place for him to go to when things got too hectic in other parts of his life. I just wanted to be even half of what he was to me, somehow.

He gave me so much. And he didn't even know it.

Toeing my feet into my sandals, I padded my way into his big, open-concept kitchen, using the stove-top light to search his fridge for eggs, bacon and toast.

I'd make us a few sandwiches and then go to the café down the street for coffee. Hopefully, he wouldn't even notice I'd gone. The image of him waking to find me gone sprang to mind and I shook it off, hoping he had a bit more trust in me now.

I wouldn't run off on him, again. I knew I'd have to tell him everything, all of my past and my secrets, in order for us to work.

And I *really* wanted us to work.

Cracking two eggs into a pan, I took some bread out to toast while they were cooking and tried not to think about the inevitable alternative. Now that I'd decided to take a chance on this man, I didn't want to worry about the 'what ifs' anymore.

If we didn't work out? I'd find a way to survive it.

Lord knows, I'd been through worse.

18

ASHER

*F*uck, something smelled good. Opening my eyes, my first thought went to the beauty that shared my bed last night.

I'd thought we were done. That I'd pushed too far, too fast. That I spooked her. But my angel wasn't so easily spooked. Yes, she was scared to let a man into her life, her heart. I didn't know much about her past, just that she'd had some issues with drugs during the last few years. Blake hadn't gone into detail. Now, I was glad he hadn't.

I didn't want to hear the details of her past from him, or anyone, really. I wanted those carefully hidden secrets to come from her lips, with trust shining in her eyes; trust I'd earned after she'd pushed me away like she had.

Rolling onto my side, I reached for her waist, wanting another feel of her before I had to get up, first for the gym, as I did every morning, and then work. I had an urge to text my brothers and tell them to make do without me today, wanting to spend a day with my angel. But before I could ask that of her, I realized that her side of the bed was not only empty, but cold, as if she hadn't been in bed for quite some time.

I'm going to tie her to my fucking bed next time.

I thought she wanted to give us a fighting chance. I thought she was sorry for lying, for pushing me away so harshly. But yet again, I woke up to find her *gone*. Fear licked up my spine as I sat up and dropped my head in my hands, pulling at my hair as panic and annoyance thundered through me, my chest shaking with the force of it.

No. She didn't get to do this to us again. She didn't get to run back to her lonely life before me and convince herself she was doing the right thing by staying away, again. I hadn't fared well during the long three weeks we'd spent apart after she'd pushed me away. Call me selfish, but I didn't want to have to miss her again.

I didn't want her to be gone, for Christ's sake!

"Tayla!" My roar was booming, guttural, a chant, a prayer that she was still here, somewhere. That she hadn't left me again.

"Come eat, Ash. It's almost ready!" I thought I was imagining it when her soft, sweet voice met my ears but that sound, her voice, I couldn't have conjured it up.

It was *real*.

She was here.

Thank fuck.

Not bothering with a shirt, I dragged my boxers over my now soft shaft, the arousal for her that I'd awoken with long gone, due to the fuckin' crippling fear that finding she was missing had caused.

I was going to tie her to my bed and then we'd see

117

about breakfast. This would be the last time she escaped my bed without my knowledge.

"*Come here,*" I growled at her, my face marred with a scowl and my eyes dark with what I was sure looked like anger. I knew I should try to be soft with her, not wanting to scare her away, again. But these emotions inside of me wouldn't let me.

I needed her. Fuck, how I needed her.

In my *bed.* My *life.* My *home.* With a ring on her finger so she couldn't leave, ever again. That would be happening soon, I resolved.

I got my first look at her as she turned my way, her long, blonde hair spread over her back as she placed two egg sandwiches onto a plate, bacon sizzling in the pan beside her.

My girl could cook, it seemed. I was thankful for it, since I usually just ordered out most days, only having home-cooked meals when Elsa or Ally came over for dinner. The women in my life were amazing cooks. It wasn't a surprise that my angel would be any different.

"Ash? Are you –"

"Please, Angel. Come here. Take the bacon off so it doesn't burn."

Her wide, hazel eyes filled with confusion as she nodded slowly, unsure of why I was being so firm with her this morning. *She didn't get it.* She didn't understand what waking up to see her gone did to me.

I knew we hadn't made any promises that night we met, but I didn't think she'd be gone before I even had the chance to take her on a real, proper date. I'd fallen for her that first night. I was gone over her, there was no question about that.

I couldn't lose her now. My eyes stung suddenly with emotion, something I hadn't felt much of since my mom died when I was a teen. I didn't like messy things like relationships in my life. I didn't like feeling like a pussy over a woman. But Tayla was worth it. She was *mine*.

I heard the sizzling stop as she moved the pan to an unlit burner and her soft footsteps as she approached me.

"Asher, I'm sorry..."

"You will be." I leaned down and grabbed for her little waist, hoisting her up and over my shoulder before I secured an arm around her already flailing legs and turned back toward my room.

We would eat later.

Right now, she had some apologizing to do.

I could feel her confusion as she looked up at me, swaying on her feet as I set her down in my room. *Our* room, if I had my way.

"Do you realize what you've done to me, Angel?"

"What? Ash, I was just —"

"No," I groaned, unable to stop my insistent cock from tenting my boxers as I caged her in to the wall by the bed, her hot little body pressing into my chest and her legs parting just a bit as my knee pressed between them.

"Don't ever leave me again." Dropping my head, I licked a hot path up her throat to nibble on her ear, knowing my beard was tickling her skin from the way she jumped and squirmed beneath me.

"Asher! That tickles— "My angel quit talking when I took her chin in my hand, dipping my tongue into her mouth when it popped open from the pressure. Her taste hit my tongue and I groaned against her open mouth, needing her taste on my lips to calm the riot of emotions that swarmed in my head.

"Your taste is addictive, do you know that?" Laving a lick over her plump lips, I pulled back, only to reach for the tie at the back of her dress, wanting her bare tits pressing against me.

I needed her naked. *Now.*

"I was making us breakfast, Ash." She barely said the words, they were little more than a whisper. But I heard them. Pulling her in close, I held her pretty face in both hands and let the love I already felt for her show in my eyes.

"I won't have you running out on me again. I can't."

"It wasn't like that this time."

"This time?" A cynical laugh left me and, peeling her sleep shirt over her head, I just shook my head at her, amazed that she didn't see how badly I needed her, craved for her to be mine.

"There won't be a next time. Please, baby. For my sanity. Wake me if you need to leave." She didn't instantly agree to my terms like I'd hoped, but slowly, I watched the guilt waft over her face. I should have felt bad for putting it there. I knew she had her reasons for keeping me at arm's length. Right then? I didn't care.

I would do anything to keep her. That's how crazed she made me.

"I promise, Ash." It was a vow upon her lips and,

as she smiled softly, the trust I'd needed from her shone in her eyes. I thanked the fuckin' heavens for it.

"Now kiss me," I softly demanded and when she did, I felt it all the way in my bones.

19

TAYLA

*M*y body ached deliciously as I opened my eyes for the second time today. After our little fight and a cold breakfast, we found ourselves in bed again; our need for each other was that strong.

I didn't remember ever being this sexual in any of my other relationships. Especially not with Trent. But sex with Asher was different. It was... *everything*.

He didn't just fuck me. He treasured me, loved me, even.

My heart stopped for a beat in my chest at that word, knowing that thinking it about him, so early on, could be a dangerous, reckless thing. But as soon as those thoughts came into my mind, I pushed them away.

I knew Asher wouldn't hurt me. I knew it in my soul.

Hurting me was the last thing he wanted to do. Just like I wouldn't want to hurt the big alpha male who lay next to me now. He was making me feel so many things I never thought I wanted or deserved. If I wasn't careful, I'd fall in love before I knew it.

"Angel, wake up." Turning my head toward his deep voice, I realized he wasn't sleeping like I'd thought. He was perched on his desk chair, his hands steeple over his forehead, those long, tanned fingers curling around his head as if in pain.

My chest ached at the sight. "Ash..."

"I fucked up, baby." Unease pelted through me at his words and, sitting up, I reached for him as my skin prickled with panic.

Was he changing his mind about us? About us?

"What's wrong?" He sat on the edge of the bed next to me and the steel in his eyes had my worry heightening. Whatever it was, we'd face it together. *Right?*

"I forgot the condom last night, baby. I was so focused on you, us and I just..." The look in his eyes was something I didn't think I could ignore, even if I had the choice. Worry. Fear. Guilt.

As he squeezed my hands tight, I wasn't sure how to feel. Panic and fear were filling my veins and my mind was imagining the worst case scenario – one in which I was pregnant and lost, without any money to support the baby I wanted, but couldn't have...

Again.

Another part of me, though, knew Asher wouldn't let that happen.

That didn't mean I was anywhere near ready for that eventuality.

The idea of going through all of it again...

"No," I whispered, more to myself than Asher.

No, no, no, no. I couldn't – wouldn't – do it again.

My baby boy was a part of me, the hole he'd left in my now broken heart one I would never be able to fill. Not with Asher. Not with a shiny new job. Not even with another child. Spencer was my miracle, a way out of the dark place my life once was. I wouldn't subject another baby to the same fate.

"Tay..."

"Don't, Asher." Pulling away from his hold on me, I turned over on my side, knowing that if I looked into his eyes, I would have to tell him the truth – that this wasn't the first time I'd had a scare like this.

Closing my eyes tightly, I tried to calm myself down, knowing that worrying about it wasn't going to make the situation any better. Asher had forgotten to wear a condom. It was an easy mistake. I shouldn't be so hard on him, but I didn't know how to stop.

I couldn't do it again. *Couldn't.*

"Don't shut me out." His words were anguished, the regret so evident in his voice, I could feel it whispering over my skin. The bed dipped as he curled his long, muscular body around mine, an arm circling my waist as his lips pressed against the side of my neck, seeking forgiveness without words.

"I was careless with you. Be mad. Yell at me. Don't give me this silence. Fuck, I can't take it, Tayla." Pressing my fingers into his that were holding my waist, I knew he deserved the truth. About everything. Me. My past. Spencer.

"I have to tell you something."

"You don't have to." His response was quick, but I could hear the sincerity in it. He wasn't going to push me for answers, details of my past I'd rather forget than relive.

"I want to." Turning in his arms so I could look at him, I reached up and clasped his face in my hands. Ignoring the flash of arousal touching him brought, I focused on the courage I'd need to tell him this.

"Tell me you'll listen. Tell me this won't change anything."

I was begging him to be patient with me, believe me when anyone else would write me off.

If anyone would believe me, it was him.

My Asher.

"*Nothing* could change my feelings for you, Angel. Nothing."

Grabbing his hands in mine, I nodded, believing him. I just hoped that when the time came, he would believe me right back.

20

ASHER

"I wasn't always like this, Asher. I need you to know that. At one time, I had dreams, a path I wanted my life to take. I wanted to own the flower shop with my mom and dreamed of finding love, having children and having a career, too. I thought the sky was the limit and I couldn't wait to finish my degree and move back here to start my life. But a little over a year ago, that all changed." My angel paused, her eyes dropping from mine and going to her lap as she struggled to collect herself.

She thought that I'd think less of her because of her past, but that wasn't possible. In a sense, I understood it, because everyone had a vice, whether it was drugs, a bad habit or even an unhealthy relationship. I was sure that if I looked real hard at my own life, I'd find I had a few of those, too. It didn't make her weak. *Not by a long shot.* My Tayla was so fucking strong and I hated that she didn't see it. She thought of herself as weak and I knew it would take a lot more than my insistence for her to see it.

That dark, sad past of hers hurt her deeply, it was evident the soul-crushing sadness I saw in her eyes, now. Maybe talking about it would help her. Maybe it wouldn't.

Without knowing what her secrets were, I couldn't know the answer. What I did know, though, was that her secrets wouldn't change my feelings for her. I was gone over her and needed her in my life; one way or another. Even if all she could ever give me was the physical, I'd take it. I would take what I could get with her and barter for the rest of it. She'd see it eventually.

We were *it*.

"Go ahead, baby." Looking up at me as I spoke, she gazed me for a long minute before she nodded, squeezing my fingers between hers as if she was steeling herself for the truth she was about to let spill from those pretty lips of hers.

"I met Trent while I was at a birthday party for one of my friends in senior year. I remember thinking he was cute, in a boy-next-door sort of way. He had this way about him that put me at ease and my nervousness about being at the party went away when he walked up to me. I was never one for parties." My hands were in fists at my sides as she continued, describing a man she'd met that seemed to be perfect and without flaw.

It was bullshit, because that shit just wasn't real. Men weren't perfect, no matter how much their women hoped they were. Everyone has flaws and makes mistakes. It's a fact of life. I could feel the rage creeping through my veins at the thought that this man had mistreated her and knew I had to prepare myself for it, but was still secretly hoping I wouldn't have to.

"It was good between us at first. He was the first

man I'd dated seriously, so I didn't see the signs before it was too late. I was so stupid, Ash." The cracks in her voice fucking broke me. *Shit.*

"Hey. Come here." I tugged her real close and, gently taking hold of her chin, I tilted it up until I could see her face. Seeing the tears in her eyes was too much. My chest ached and all I wanted was to take her pain away, no matter the cost. She was so sweet, so good, so beautiful.

She deserved so much more from her life than what she'd been dished out.

"Ah, shit. Don't do this to me." I buried my face into her thick, blonde locks and inhaled her sweet, cherry scent and just *held* her. Her small hands found purchase around my neck and my mouth was against her cheek, breathing her in. It was a reminder for the both of us.

We may have lived different lives and yeah, there were secrets separating us. But this connection we had? It was real.

"I'm sorry," I breathed into her skin and felt her body soften against me.

"You don't have to tell me the rest. I want you to know that, Tayla. I know how hard this must be for you and it's hurting you, I can see that. I don't ever want to intentionally cause you pain."

I gently cupped her tear-stained cheeks and dropped my forehead to hers, praying that she wouldn't push me away.

I was a strong person, but when she pushed me away and ran that time, it was like taking my heart straight from my chest. We may have only just met, but she was mine.

All. Fucking. Mine.

If only she knew that.

"I want to tell you, Ash. I want you to know everything. It's time."

I nodded, not sure if it was the best thing for her anymore.

As she placed her fingers on my jaw, the touch reassured me and, pulling marginally away from her, I reached for her hands again, hoping to hell I could fix whatever pain filled her eyes as she continued.

"I didn't see it until it was too late. He was so good at making me feel special, as if I was the only girl in the world to him. It started off with weed, a joint he'd roll up and pass to me. And it just went downhill from there. Soon enough, he had me high on whatever needle he could get his hands on and passed me around to all his junkie friends..."

"Motherfucker!" Rage. That's all I felt. White, hot, angry rage. I had the instant need to wrap my fingers around her ex's throat and squeeze the life out of him. Tayla was such a kind, loyal, beautiful person and this jerk-off, whoever he was, had taken advantage of her. If I got my hands on him...

"Asher..." Her voice was softer now, regret bleeding through and I cursed under my breath, forcing back my anger, replacing it with the need to comfort her.

All that mattered was getting her through this.

When the time was right, I'd get his name out of her and make sure he was behind bars, where he belonged. Until then, Tayla was my priority.

"I knew he was into the hard stuff and that he wanted me to try it, too. I didn't know why, because I told him I'd help him get clean. Whenever I did, he got really angry. Trent was really proud; he didn't want to be viewed as weak and he loved the high."

"That doesn't surprise me for a minute, Angel. You have such a big heart."

A slight smile spread her lips and she leant forward and kissed my cheek gently before taking a deep breath and telling me the rest.

"When I found out I was pregnant, I didn't know what to think. I'd always been careful. Always. But there were plenty of nights I was too out of it to know what was happening and the guys he brought around weren't exactly gentlemen."

Wait, what?

She'd had a baby? And she was only telling me this now? My head was spinning but I didn't dare let her go. I needed to know the rest now, knowing that whatever it was, it might change us.

I always thought I would have kids someday, once I'd gotten my head out of my ass and settled down with a nice girl. I had no doubt in my mind that if she had a child, I would do the right thing and take care of them both.

I was way too invested now. Walking away wasn't an option.

"I wasn't ready, Ash. I was only twenty-one and by the time I found out, I was using anytime I could. That high was my best friend. It was an escape I needed at the time." I didn't know what to say. It was a lot to take in but, more than that, I was astonished. She'd obviously kept the ones that she loved away during that time in her life. She was on her own and this asshole had taken advantage of that.

Tayla lifted her head from where it rested on my

shoulder and looked at me, a mix of fear and hope filling her hazel eyes.

"*Asher*?"

"Yeah, I'm still listening."

"Say something, please." Her voice was a plea, a desperation.

I held her as close as possible and nodded, still unsure what to say. I settled for the truth.

"You're so fucking strong, Tayla." The look in her eyes told me she didn't believe my words, but that was okay. I had plenty of time to convince her.

My mouth ghosted over hers, earning me a sharp gasp from her pretty red lips. Maybe she thought I'd be angry that she kept such a big secret from me, but I couldn't be. Because knowing she trusted me with them meant every- fuckin'-thing.

"Kiss me," she begged me, her hushed, breathy voice making me rock hard in seconds. *How could I say no?*

I couldn't and as I realized that, she reached up, tangling her hands in my hair and tugging me down fully to her lips. I groaned deep in my throat, growling when I smelled the cherry lip balm she always used on those lips of hers.

I had to have a taste. Pulling her lower lip into my mouth, I pulled at the skin and loved the moan for more that my angel gave me. Her hands were gripping my shoulders tightly, her knees around my waist and that sweet, tight pussy of hers hugging my dick over my slacks and her sweat pants. Goddamn.

"Ash," she whimpered against my mouth, pulling at my hair in her need for more and I grinned, grinding her hips against mine as my hunger for her grew and grew. She may have thought telling me of her past would stop my feelings for her, but it seemed it was the exact opposite; I craved her even more.

"Now." I cleared my throat, willing my hard-on down so that I could figure out the rest. Now that she'd told me about her past, I was even more determined to take care of her and love her like she deserved. "Tell me the rest."

Sweeping her hair away from her eyes, I looked down at her and, after a few seconds, she nodded.

"I knew I wasn't ready to be a mom, not even close. I was in such a dark place and even if I'd gotten clean, would I be able to give my son everything he'd need? I found a couple through a friend of my dad's and after Spencer was born, I signed the paperwork."

Her voice was low and shaky and her eyes were dark with a pain I couldn't even fathom. She must have been so scared, all alone and without the support she should have had during that time in her life. She was toying with the buttons on my shirt, her eyes pleading for my understanding and, without a doubt in my mind, I gave it to her. I would have given her anything she needed, all she had to do was ask.

During the hardest time in her life, she had been forced to make a decision, one not for herself, but for the unborn child she was bringing into the world. It was a selfless choice, one I was sure was difficult for her to come to.

I wouldn't judge her for it, not when I knew how strong and compassionate Tayla was. She must have wanted her son so much, but because of circumstances outside of her control, she had made the only choice she thought she had. I was so damn proud of her.

"I'm so sorry, Tay. So sorry." Pressing her face into

the crook of my neck, she nodded against me, burying her nose against my skin. I felt her breathing me in before she slowly drew away and looked up at me with wide, tearful eyes.

The look in her eyes shattered me.

2 1

TAYLA

"*I* miss him so much." Asher's face went slack and the warmth spread in his irises, comforting me instantly.

"I know you do, Tayla. Jesus, I wish I could bring him back to you. That's what you want, isn't it? To be with him again."

Nodding, I clutched him closer, desperate for an anchor. He was my anchor.

"Yes. No. I don't know, Asher. He was so beautiful, so perfect...I only had a few minutes with him. But he went to a good family. They'll make sure he has everything he needs and more. I know that." I eased my hands through his dark brown locks, needing the traction his hard, muscled, protective embrace gave me.

"Tell me about them." I pulled back then, knowing he was trying to help me. I hadn't thought about Charlie and her wife in so long, it sort of seemed like another life ago. She'd come to me after they'd taken my sweet boy away. Wanting to assure me. Wanting to comfort me.

How could she be so kind to me, when I was so

selfish? I was giving up my son. I was all he had in the world. All he knew.

And I was abandoning him.

"Angel, stop thinking. Just tell me." He knew me so well. *Too well,* my inner voice told me. But he was what I needed. Between his insisting of our connection, his virility in loving me between the sheets and of course, his kindness, I'd fallen.

And it scared the crap out of me. Because needing someone like I needed Asher could break me, I knew that from experience. But as he waited for me to tell him about my son, my baby boy, I couldn't be afraid, anymore.

Because more than anything, this man was my safety net.

"It was a couple. Charlie, she was really nice. Kind. Beautiful. I knew she was used to taking care of her own, being the strong one among others. I trusted her the moment I met her. She wants to be a vet, she told me that. Said she's settling for working at a local shelter for now. I had no doubt she'd make that dream come true, though." I opened my eyes and looked up at Asher.

My Asher. But it was like he was a million miles away. Thinking and lost in a memory, not truly here with me.

"Ash?"

"Yeah." His voice was gruff, deep. I recoiled, unsure. Was this the beginning of the end? *Was he just staying with me out of pity?*

"Sorry, Tayla. Lost in thought. It's not you, baby." His hand gripped mine as he spoke and my worries slipped away and I *believed* him. Wholeheartedly.

Somewhere, somehow, he'd earned my trust. *I just prayed he wouldn't break it.*

"What about her partner?"

"Ally. Or Allison, I think. She's an artist. She has this big family, I guess. Charlie said something like four siblings, who all have their own children by now. Crazy, I know." I laughed and it was like I could breathe again. The pain and the shakes and the worries were passing. I felt my body being relieved of some of the heaviness I'd carried around with me for so long, just through talking about them.

Asher's mouth pressed to my forehead, bringing me back to the moment and I smiled. A real smile. A genuine one.

"We're going to get you through this. You believe that?" Clutching his hands with mine, I nodded.

"I do."

∼

One bath, two low-dose aspirin and one long, languid nap later, I was feeling much more myself. The weight of keeping my past, my addiction and Spencer from Asher had fell away from my shoulders and it felt like I could breathe easy, now.

"Tip your head back." His voice, smooth as silk, next to my ear.

I complied, letting him work his purposeful hands through my hair as he washed it for me. I never thought having someone shampoo my hair would be sexy, but with him? It was.

Asher hummed low in his throat and I opened my eyes and met his softened gaze, saw the corners of his mouth lifting in a ghost of a smile. As I looked at him, though, I noticed the expression didn't quite reach his eyes. In the few hours since I told him about Charlie and the family who'd adopted Spencer, his eyes had been darker – like he was hiding something from me.

Paranoid, much?

Was it really just that, though? Had I said too much, too soon? It was no surprise that I had trouble opening up to those around me. Especially men.

I'd been with one man in my life and God, he'd done a number on me.

But Asher didn't let me distance myself from him, even though I'd tried.

He was too damn stubborn, pig-headed and persistent with me. I both liked it and despised it. It meant I couldn't get away with shielding myself from him, or pushing him away. At the end of the day, I knew he'd be there for me.

Through thick and thin.

It didn't matter what happened or how massively I managed to mess up my life. This stubborn man wouldn't be dissuaded. Once he knew what he wanted, he went after it.

And if the last few weeks of knowing him had taught me anything, it was that he didn't give up easily.

I touched his face with hesitant fingertips, wanting to take away the darkness, the coldness I saw in his eyes right then. It wasn't directed at me. Whenever he looked at me, a softness came to his face that was unmistakable. I knew he cared about me and the way he looked at me...

It felt like so much more. No one had ever looked at me the way he did.

Like I was cherished.

Like I was wanted.

Like I was special.

"Is something wrong?" I asked, rubbing my fingers over the roughness of his jaw, where he'd either forgotten to shave or had chosen not to; I wasn't sure. His stubble felt good against my skin, reminding me of the way it felt when he kissed me. It scratched my skin as he ravaged my mouth, selfish, taking no prisoners in his claiming of my lips.

I ached, my stomach tightening and my pussy clenching beneath the warm water of my bath. If I closed my eyes, I was sure I could still feel him inside me, drawing himself through my slick folds as if we had all the time in the world. In a lot of ways, we had.

That was, until I'd run away.

"No, Angel. I'm just thinking about some things. It's not you." He reached down and cupped my face in his hands and his touch was like a buzz of a microphone.

My skin pebbled in goosebumps and my chest tightened in anticipation of what he would say, how he would touch me next. I craved him more than any drug, any pill, any liquor I'd ever had.

He was my savior, my protector but, more than anything, he was the man I wanted. No, *needed*.

"Are you ready to get out now?" Nodding, I smiled softly, not wanting him to know how depraved my thoughts were. I was ready to jump him, I realized.

As Asher lifted me out of the tub and held me close, my ear pressed to his hard, beautiful, bare chest, I found myself remembering what my sponsor told me when I left the program where I got clean.

Let love in, Tayla. If you don't, the addiction may always have a hold on you. And I know you're stronger than that.

I was stronger. Maybe I needed to hit rock bottom to realize that, or maybe having gone through what I had was what I'd needed to finally open my heart again.

Maybe Asher hadn't been a distraction, like I'd thought when we'd first met. He was so good, so strong and determined that I was worth the trouble I brought to his life. What if he was sent into my life not to tempt my will for sobriety, but to ensure my happiness?

What if Asher was the one I needed to save myself?

"Easy now," he murmured as he slowly set me down on the bed and my hands, urgent and of their own will, hung tightly to his shoulders. I didn't want to let go.

It was childish to think that if I didn't let go of him physically, I wouldn't lose him in a greater sense. That was what my heart told me, though.

"Lie down with me, Ash."

"I don't think that's a good idea, Tayla."

He shook his head roughly, turning away from me so I couldn't see whatever he was feeling in his eyes. My stomach took a nose-dive and all of the warmth and excitement about what lay ahead for us dissipated in the wake of his easy refusal.

It was obvious to me, then.

He didn't want me anymore.

I turned over quickly, reaching down and pulling the comforter on his bed over my shoulders, before I buried my face in his pillow and hoped he didn't hear my sniffles as I let a few tears freely fall. A moment later, it didn't matter because I heard the firm sound of the door as he closed it behind him.

I'd never felt so alone.

22

ASHER

*S*pencer was her son.

How was that even possible? I shook my head roughly and dragged urgent, unsteady hands through my hair in an effort to calm myself before I did something crazy – like tell my sister or my angel the truth.

She was finally opening up to me and I knew no matter how strong she felt right now, she wasn't ready for this. I was very close with my family; always had been. How was I supposed to keep this secret from them, or her?

Fuck you, Fate. I ground my teeth and clenched my jaw, needing the slight pain it gave me in order to get my bearings. Walking out onto the balcony of my apartment, I dropped a hand to my pocket and pulled out my cell phone. I punched in the security code and scrolled through my contacts until I saw my brother's information. If anyone could talk me down and make me see reason, it was Ben.

"Hey. I figured you'd be calling me today."

"Oh, really?" I laughed, a strained one I hoped he didn't pick up on.

141

He was my big brother. Of course he did.

"What's up, Asher?" *I was fucked*. But I didn't say that.

"I need your advice." Ben was always my first call when I felt lost in my life. When things didn't make sense and I wanted to burn every shred of it to flames, he was the one that got through to me, grounded me, even.

While Luke was the goof, always making us laugh when we needed it most, Ben was the logical one, always thinking things through before he made choices; something I often wished I did. And Ally – Ally was the artist out of all of us. She always had a smile on her face and a project in the works and I'm sure my brothers would agree that she's the most dedicated out of all of us.

I wasn't really sure where I fell among them, but did know that if I was going to figure out what to do about this situation, I needed their help.

"She give you the time of day yet?"

"Yeah. She's finally opening up, thank fuck. I thought I'd have to tie her down to get her to talk." Ben's loud, hearty laugh sounded in my ear and I shook my head at him, though of course he couldn't see it.

"You just want to tie her down, man."

"Probably." Another forced laugh. I was getting good at masking them.

"She has a son, Ben. She gave him up and he was adopted by a lesbian couple." *One I knew*.

"Lucky kid." The humor in his voice was laced with sarcasm. Leave it to my brother to make a damn joke when I was losing my fuckin' mind.

"Shut up, man. This is serious."

"Just imagine, how much boob action that sucker will get..."

My brother, folks. He was the smartass out of all of us when he felt like it.

"Alright, I'm done. How are you dealing with all this?" His voice had grown somber, clear worry evident in his tone. He may have been a goof and a wise-ass, but he was also the most genuine, loyal person I knew. If anyone could give me some clarity, right about then, it would be him.

"Honestly? I understand. I don't know what I'd do in the situation if it were me and it's really not my place to judge her. She could have told me she was a murderer and I'd still love her." *Fuck,* I did love her. *Madly.*

I could honestly say I had absolutely zero doubts when it came to Tayla. She was the best part of my days and the one I needed to sleep next to at night. Of course I loved her. I hadn't said it, because I wasn't a complete fool. My feelings for her would spook her and I'd already managed to do that once before. If we had any chance of making it, I had to keep my lid shut and take shit slow.

I just hoped she didn't run, again.

"Does she know?"

"Nah. I don't want to scare her off."

"Yeah, that's probably smart. So what about the baby? Does she want to get him back, or..." He was getting right to the point but I needed to get this out of my system, so for once, I was thankful for my brother's impatience.

"You may want to sit down for this, Ben." Lord knew, it threw me for a fuckin' loop.

"Shit. Out with it." I inhaled a deep breath,

dropped my head into the hand that wasn't holding the phone and told him the worst of it.

"His name is *Spencer*."

"*Fuck*."

"Yeah."

"Like, our nephew, Spencer?"

"Yep." I stretched out my neck, trying to get the sudden tension out of my muscles. How my sister was going to handle this news, I didn't fucking know.

"Ally..."

"Yeah. Tell me about it. I need you to tell me what to do, man. I'm out of my mind right now." I sounded desperate and I realized I was. I was on the brink, unsure of what to do. I always relied on the truth, the facts when making decisions, but telling Tayla the truth *now...*?

I wasn't sure she could handle it. *If I was in her shoes, could I?*

I really didn't think so.

It wasn't only that I'd be telling her where her son was, but also that the family that took him in and adopted him as one of their own was mine.

Would I have to choose between her and my family?

Was that even a choice?

Could I cut them out of my life if it meant having her with me?

I didn't have any answers. Not even one.

"You need to tell Ally. She deserves to know before shit hits the fan."

"And what am I supposed to tell Tayla? She's going to want him back. She misses him." I felt it when she spoke of him. If the specifics were different,

I would have done nothing but look for him if that was what she wanted.

I would marry her little ass and raise her son as my own.

But my sister... She'd wanted to be a mother more than anything.

It hadn't been easy for her and Charlie to find a surrogate and, when they finally did, it was like she could smile again. She'd spent so long taking care of us and being the glue for our family during the hardest times we'd faced. She and Charlie deserved happiness.

Did that mean Tayla didn't? *Of course not.* I just didn't know what to do.

I wanted to put the girl in there first, over everything in the world.

This was my *sister*. How could I choose happiness for one, but not both of them?

"You know our sister. She's the most caring person we know. Talk to her first, tell Dad and go from there. Yeah?"

Like I said, level-headed.

"Yeah, brother. Thanks."

"Just remember, this isn't on you. She'll push you away, be angry...but none of this is your fault, Asher. You'll find your way through it. Be patient with her."

Fuck. He was probably right. I just wished I knew a way to shield Tayla from getting hurt by all of this. It seemed no matter what I did, she'd be hurt.

I hated that.

"Yeah, I hear you. I'm going to go and talk to her. See you later." I spoke quietly as I opened my bedroom door slowly, knowing she was probably asleep by now.

"That sounds like a good idea. Good luck."

Hanging up the phone, I pulled the door closed behind me and padded, barefoot back into the room, not wanting to wake her just yet. We'd had a long day. And my angel needed sleep if she was going to keep up with me and my constant need for her. It thrummed to life inside me as I climbed into bed with her and lifted the covers, my fingers seeking out warm, soft skin that felt like home every time I felt it against mine.

My chest ached with a sudden, sharp pain and something that felt like panic seized my heart and squeezed it in a vise-like grip. What the...?

Pulling the covers back from the pillows of my bed, I let my hand fall against the sheets and the spot where she had been lying when I left her was now empty and cold.

Fuck!

My angel was *gone*.

23

TAYLA

TWELVE HOURS LATER

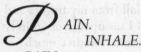

*P*AIN.
INHALE.
PAIN.
Exhale.

The thick, fragrant smell of the smoke of the blunt wedged between my dry, chapped lips overwhelmed my senses and I hated the fact that I needed it.

I needed it so badly. I was a slave to the smoke, the drug, the *high.*

Agitation crept up my spine like a sickening wind on my back and I clenched my hair in my fingers, pulling at the smooth strands as I tried, yet again, to get a hold of myself. I hadn't always been this girl. The girl lingering on a street corner, scratching at her skin in an incessant need for her next fix. The girl who always hurt the ones she loved. The girl who always hurt and disappointed and ran away from her responsibilities.

I used to be different. *Good.* Barely opening my eyes, my gaze caught on the elastic band marks, covering my inner arm, red from being wrapped around too tight as I pushed a needle into my skin, yet again. I never wanted to, again. But here I was, submitting to that high once more. I used to be stronger than this. Hadn't I?

A student.

A daughter.

A sister.

I used to know which was way was up, what was right and what was irrefutably wrong.

I used to be better.

Before Trent. Before Spencer. Before the drugs.

I let the offending blunt fall from my fingers and onto the dirty cement ground I sat upon, not entirely knowing how I had gotten there. I didn't much remember anything, if I thought about it. I remembered Asher, though.

He was so good, so real...

After our night together, I knew I couldn't lie to myself anymore.

I wasn't the girl he thought I was. He thought I was worth saving, but he didn't see who I really was.

I was selfish and masochistic.

I knew if I went down this road again, I'd fall prey to the urges that inhabited my head and cooled my bloodstream.

It was just easier.

To be weak. To be broken. To be this.

But the very second, I let myself love him, *need* him, I realized how easy it would be for him to hurt me. But, for some crazy reason, I just didn't believe he would.

I'd sat there and told him everything – about the

drugs, Spencer, Trent, even. Things I hadn't even confided in my own parents or my sister.

I trusted them, but with Asher, I knew I wouldn't be judged or made to feel like my choices defined me and who I was to him. He accepted me, flaws and all. I could be silly and weird with him. I could cry in front of him and he wouldn't see me as anything less than strong, as he never failed to remind me I was.

I felt safe with this man and I didn't care anymore if it was too soon or too fast to feel the way I felt. We just... fit.

But I'd been wrong about that, too. Because the moment I bared myself to him, he pulled away from me, not even wanting to sleep next to me, instead going into the living room to sleep on his frumpy old couch.

It had crushed me. Not because he slept on the couch. But because he had made it perfectly, painfully clear that he didn't want me anymore.

Maybe he never had.

That pain, that excruciating, desperation-causing, heart-breaking pain, drove me to do what I was best at, what felt safe to me. I *ran*.

As if of its own will, my hand went to the base of my neck, where the necklace Scarlet gave me hung loosely under the neckline of my blouse. It was a pendant with a small birthstone placed in it; *my* birthstone. It was a crescent heart and Scarlet had kept the other half of the necklace. It was our way of always being with one another, even when we weren't. I remembered that day so clearly, as if it was yesterday. My sister knew me better than anyone and so, on the day I'd come home from rehab the last time, she'd given me this. She'd told me that if I ever felt alone, as

I often did, all I had to do was look at this necklace and I'd know she was there with me.

After my baby boy's birth, it was really hard for me to accept affection from family or friends around me. It was too hard to let myself and my emotions go and so I kept them all bottled up inside. I think it was easier for me at the time, in the long run, though it was the thing that broke me. I couldn't stand to even live with myself afterwards, hating myself for the selfish decision I'd made when it came to my son.

I've been alone ever since.

Clutching my pendant tightly with my fingers, I realized it was a conscious choice I was making for myself. Because there was a man who wanted to be there for me, though I had never allowed him to be. He said I didn't have to go through this alone and, if I was honest with myself, I knew I didn't *want* to be alone.

Not anymore.

Even if he didn't want me anymore, we had something to fight for.

I would be a fool not to fight for him, wouldn't I?

I rushed to my feet as the realization settled inside me. Swaying on shaky, unsteady legs, I stilled, waiting until the dizziness within my mind calmed. It had been hours since my last hit and I knew I'd need another one soon.

But another hit wasn't what I needed right then. Not even the dwindling buzz pulling through my chest had me wanting it. There was a different high I craved, one I knew would last and last. One with a broad, full mouth and a slight twang to his deep, honeyed voice.

One that called me Angel and calmed me with just one look.

Maybe he didn't want me. Maybe I was a fool for wanting to go to him, when I was in this dark, hopeless place.

But I had to try. *Asher.*

I needed Asher.

24

ASHER

"*G*et off me, I'm *fine!*" I grappled for traction on the floor beneath me as my brothers held me back, keeping me immobile. *Fuckers,* I thought to myself and the only reason I didn't say it to their faces was because I didn't want to give them the satisfaction. It had been almost eight hours since Tayla had disappeared on me– had run as if staying with me was the worst kind of fate.

I had pushed her, *again,* to let me in, let me *love* her and what had she done? *She'd run from me.* I'd searched for her everywhere I could and still my angel was nowhere I could find.

What kind of man did that make me? That I couldn't find my woman when she obviously needed to be *anything* but alone?

This was my last stop in my search of her – Harlots' Tavern, a local bar Blake told me she'd frequented before the last occasion she was admitted to rehab. But she wasn't fucking here.

Where the fuck was she?

"You're not fine. You almost plummeted that guy, Ash. If she isn't here, that's not his fault." Yeah, so I probably shouldn't have had a go at the Justin Bieber lookalike kid tending the bar. The cocky shit had it coming when he didn't give me the answers I needed, though.

After my service overseas, I could keep my calm in even the highest stress situations. Heat, cold, hunger, thirst; I'd learned to live without even the barest necessities.

But for some reason, not being able to find my angel was the thing that had me losing my edge. The frightened look in her eyes when she'd told me about Spencer earlier today told me that I was too far gone, now. She was a part of me now, engrained in my *motherfuckin'* skin. She didn't need me to be whole, but I needed her. *Desperately.*

That girl was my oxygen. My sanity. My salvation.

She was the one I'd be coming home to, for the rest of my damn life if I had my way.

I just needed to *find* her. This was all on me and if I didn't get to her before...Ben's hands left my arms as a strong shudder racked my body.

I just had to find her.

"Let's go, Ash. Maybe she's wound up at home by now."

"Yeah," I muttered, disbelief clouding my head. "Maybe."

I was barely able to stay under the speed limit as I rushed back to my apartment. I was planning to grab a change of clothes and head toward Tayla's family's home as soon as I could possibly get there. It was unlikely that she'd go there if she knew I'd be looking for her, but I was still headed that way. One way or another, she was going to have to deal with me.

I was not going to give up on her. Maybe she was expecting that, since she had gone through so much heartache in her young life. She'd just have to realize that wouldn't be the case with us.

Not ever.

Because I loved her and I didn't care how long it took for her to return those feelings. *I would wait forever for the chance to love her the way she deserved to be loved.*

I pulled my truck into the small parking lot behind my building and wasted no time in grabbing my shit, pulling keys from the ignition and slamming the car door shut behind me.

I was running on autopilot, not paying attention to much else but the sound of gravel under my shoes and the pounding of my heartbeat in my ears. My hand was reaching for the door handle of the entrance when I noticed a spark of red across the parking lot. It was flimsy and colorful and as I narrowed my focus to what it was, I realized it was a scarf.

Like the scarf Tayla was wearing on our date...

Fuck! She'd been here. I almost dropped to my knees right there, on the steps of my apartment building because my chest was crushing in on itself at the thought of anything happening to my angel. I couldn't live with myself if I knew something happened while she'd been running from *me*. I forced a deep breath to fill my lungs, and then another, not allowing myself to move from where I stood until I'd calmed down enough to make a plan.

Emotion clouding my judgment wasn't something I could risk.

Taking hold of the handle of the door once again, I opened it and mounted the stairs towards my second floor apartment. I had to keep my focus on one thing at a time, otherwise, if I let myself think about what could happen, what I could find when I finally got within touching distance of my woman, I knew I would go crazy.

As I made it into the dimly lit hallway that led to my place, I noticed someone sitting along the wall only a few feet away from my door.

Angel.

Her normally vibrant, wavy, blonde hair hung partially over her face as I drew close and only then did my knees give out, sending me dropping to my haunches directly in front of her. I was almost afraid to touch her, as fear that she was somehow hurt was ripping through my chest like the sharpest blade of a knife.

"Angel, look at me." She moved her head to the side, letting her eyes slowly flutter open until they found their way to mine. The blurriness in them told of pain and regret and the slight redness around her eyelids reminded me of my worst fear as I'd sought her out today.

She'd relapsed. I knew she'd been hurting when she told me the truth about her past, but I thought that we'd get through it, together. I could protect her from anything that wanted to cause her harm, if only she'd let me. Instead, she left me, taking my heart with her.

Kneeling in front of her, I begged whatever gods there were that I wasn't too late to help her. That I could save her, just like she'd saved me just by loving me.

She didn't have to say the words. Her love for me was evident in her gorgeous hazel eyes and beautiful, angelic smile.

I love you, Angel.

Don't leave me just yet.

We hadn't had nearly enough time.

"*Fuck*, Angel. Can you stand? Let me get you inside," I urged, feeling for her pulse to reassure myself that she really was here, that she wasn't a dream my panicked head had conjured up.

"I don't think so." Gently lifting her under the arms, I made sure to hold her by the waist in case her legs were too weak to bear her weight. She swayed against me as I picked her up off the floor, her slight weight pressing to my chest and her clammy hands finding purchase around my wrists.

"I knew I'd be safe here. I'm always safe...with you."

She'd barely gotten the words out before her body went limp in my hold, her beautiful eyes closing of their own volition as she passed out in my arms.

"Yeah," I whispered gently, not wanting to wake her as I deftly unlocked my door and lifted her against my chest, inhaling her floral scent as I held her as close as I could get her.

"I'll always keep you safe."

~

"Ash?" Her sweet voice, thick with sleep, pulled my attention from the other end of the phone and I masked a smile over my face as I met her worried stare from across the room.

"It's your sister. Give me a minute, alright?"

As if she'd only just realized what had happened and where she was, she nodded and looked away.

I hated this. I couldn't fix any of this for her. I couldn't tell her that her family would understand, because, up to now, they didn't. They were worried and hurt and angry with her for going back to the drugs that had taken her from them in the first place. And I couldn't blame them, either. They had been through this so many times before and it hurt them to see her fail, again. But she could fight her addiction.

I knew she could. She was fucking strong and even when she wasn't, she had me to lean on. She had me to be her strength, if only she would rely on me. I wasn't sure if she ever would, but I was feeling pretty hopeful after finding her here. She could have gone anywhere and sought shelter.

To her dad. To her sister. To Blake.

But, no, she'd found me. *Me.*

She may have not admitted it yet, but she knew she could trust in me. And that shit felt *damn* good.

"Let us talk to her," Scarlet said and my hackles rose, my protective instincts suddenly taking precedence over any reason I may have had. I couldn't protect her from a lot of things, but I could protect her from her family's disappointment for a while.

"She just woke up, Scarlet. How about we give you a call after she eats something?" The silence that met my ear couldn't have been good, but after a moment I heard her huff and then agree. I mumbled a quick goodbye and dropped my phone into my pants' pocket.

Approaching the bed, I let my eyes linger over her slight frame in the tank top she wore and wondered if she'd lost weight in the mere ten hours, we'd been apart. I couldn't *stand* the thought.

"Hey, Angel. How are you feeling?" Tayla blinked up at me, her slender shoulders moving ever so slightly in what looked like a shrug and I wasn't sure what to make of it. I couldn't help myself as I moved to her side and gently lifted her into my arms before sitting down where she'd been and quickly moving her into my lap. My hands sought her little hips and as my mouth trailed across her hair in the lightest of kisses, I felt her chest heave with a heavy breath.

"I'm sorry."

"Don't, Tayla." She had nothing to be sorry for. Was I angry that, instead of talking to me, she had fallen prey to the high I knew she craved... would always crave? *Hell, yes, I was.*

Would I blame her for that?

Never.

25

TAYLA

*G*od. Everything hurt.

"Ash?"

"I'm here, Angel. Sit up." I didn't have to open my eyes to see the concern in his storm-dark eyes. Despite the aches radiating through my body, the chills and the sweats and the coughs and the racing heart, I sat up against the hard wooden headboard and leaned against the surface, enjoying the cool texture against my neck.

I felt hot all over. The cold, merciless chills had taken me sometime between midnight and dawn, waking Asher up when I'd begun to shake the bed with my shivering.

He hadn't complained, though. He'd just smiled a sad, resigned smile, kissed the top of my head and pulled me as close to his warm, chiseled chest as he could get me. And I felt... safe.

Safe.

This perfect man gave me comfort and solace in a way I'd never known before and I soaked it up like the pitiful, weak addict I was. A therapist of mine once told me that it wasn't the drugs that kept me on the edge of craving. It was me.

I was an *addict*.

Something in my life had been so bad, so painful, that I couldn't deal with it on my own anymore and in order to have semblance of normalcy, I'd turned to the high I loved so much. I had an addictive streak in me a mile long, it seemed.

The first chance I could, I'd run away from this man and the crazy ways he made me feel. I didn't think I was deserving of any of it and so I'd bailed.

Fight or flight, they called it. You know what I called it? *Cowardice*.

I was in withdrawal. I knew that. Asher knew that.

I was numbing by now and only the shivers of my body remained as Asher gently tipped my chin up and placed two pills on my tongue. My eyes almost popped out of my head when I realized what he was doing. I'd told him no meds. I wasn't about to risk another relapse, not when I was finally in a safe place, where I knew I had everything I needed to squelch my addiction.

Asher. He was my antidote.

I didn't need pills, alcohol or anything else, for that matter. Because he had me.

"They're just ibuprofen, baby. *Please*. I hate seeing you like this."

My heart melted at the ardent plea in his voice and, nodding, I let the painkillers slide down my throat, aided by the cold water he helped me sip.

"My mom said you should eat. I have some left-over lasagna I'll heat up for us and then we can just veg in front of the TV. Sound good?" His rough, coarse fingertips still skated against my jaw, holding me in a gentle grasp and helping to warm my icy skin.

"Yes," I croaked, shameful annoyance filling me when I heard how utterly broken I sounded. I sipped from the glass once more and tried again.

"I'd like that." His eyes were all I could see, soft, blue depths so warm and tender, I suddenly wanted to cry. My eyes stung and I wanted to push the emotions swarming inside of my chest away but I just didn't have the strength to.

"What is it?" he crooned, his voice full of concern for me, as it had been since finding me outside his door last night. Then his hands were everywhere; On my face, cupping my cheeks earnestly. On my wrists, checking and rechecking that my pulse was still steady and I wasn't having another dizzy spell – I'd had a few last night. But then he held my waist and pulled me into his lap, where instinctively, my legs wrapped around his body.

I dipped my head into his shoulder and cried pitifully, not knowing how to deal with these emotions... ones the high helped me hide from.

Confusion.

Loneliness.

Sadness.

It all swam through me as I realized I couldn't ignore the questions that filled my still-cloudy mind. I needed to know if I'd been wrong about him. I needed to know if he could live with my brokenness, my dark past and the knowledge that I may never be without the urge to use again. I couldn't lie to myself anymore.

I loved him. *So much.* But if he really didn't want me like before, I would find a way to live with it.

I would have to.

"*Angel,* look at me. Talk to me." My face was hidden against his warm, solid chest but the clear desperation in his tone had my eyes meeting his, my defenses falling to our feet.

"A—after I told you... everything...I thought maybe something had changed. That you didn't want me anymore..."

I wasn't sure why, but the look in Asher's eyes stopped my fumbling words. The way his gaze darkened with desire, just like when we'd made love all of those times—right here in his bedroom, in fact. I saw a warmth there, too. Maybe... love?

Was I fooling myself into believing that he could love me, so soon?

"When I said nothing could change my feelings for you, I meant every damn word, Angel. You're under my skin, in my heart, in every breath I take. I don't just *want* you. I love you, Tayla. Every second of the last twenty-four hours has been hell for me, not knowing if you were safe, if you felt alone or scared when I couldn't get to you..."

Pausing, Asher pulled my face between his shaking hands, the emotion that was overpowering him pulling me under, too.

He hadn't been indifferent to me before. He was just scared.

Scared of losing me, just like I was him.

We're two peas in a pod, him and I.

The same in so many ways, desperate for the love of the other but unsure how to ask for it.

If we'd just talked to one another, divulged our fears, we wouldn't be here, with both of us hurting, losing sight of what's important.

Each other.

"I was scared, too," I murmured, letting him cradle my face and smooth his thumb over the tears that fell freely down my cheeks – tears of the sweetest relief and love for this beautiful, patient, loving man.

Anyone else would have bailed on me, thinking I was more trouble than I was worth. But Asher didn't see my flaws and my weaknesses and my broken pieces. He just saw me and loved me, in spite of it all.

"You don't have to be scared anymore. I'm not letting you out of my sight ever again." Surprised laughter bubbled up my scratchy throat and slipped from my lips and I watched, rapt, as Asher's serious expression transformed into one of happiness; relief, even.

We may be new to this whole relationship thing, but I realized in that moment that we could make each other happy.

I could make *him* happy.

"I like seeing you smile again." Reaching for his face, I rubbed a gentle hand against his stubble, reveling in the knowledge that he was mine, now.

This happiness, contentment, safety he gave me? It was everything and no one could take that away.

It was ours.

26

TAYLA

J opened my eyes slowly, unsure if I could
trust the sense of peace I felt now, in place
of the panic and pain I was so used to waking up with.
Letting myself remember the night before, I felt my
face split in a wide, elated smile, the first real one I'd
had in the last few days.

It wasn't just the withdrawal symptoms that had
caused the overwhelming emotions, the highs and
lows I'd felt the past two days. No, letting Asher in
did that. Opening myself up to all of the feelings and
memories I had pushed down deep inside of me for so
long caused a weight to lift off of my chest, and cre-
ated a sensation of peacefulness inside me that I felt
all the way down to my bones.

"Come 'ere." The half asleep demand sent a spark
of warmth through my body, one only Asher could
give me. He affected me in ways I couldn't put into
words and I wouldn't want to. Moments like these,
the quiet ones, the still ones, they were just ours. The
calm this man gave me was something I didn't want to
share with anyone, not even my busybody sister.

Turning into his waiting arms, I let myself be engulfed by his warmth, his musky *Asher* smell and the gentle yet firm way he held me; as if he was afraid to let me go for fear I would disappear again.

I'd caused that crippling fear in him by walking away from him instead of trusting him to be honest with me. It was a regret I would live with forever, but one I would make up for, now, in the present.

"You smell good, Angel." His warm breath wafted over my cheek as he whispered the words and, smiling, I nuzzled my nose into his chest and breathed him in for another easy, peaceful moment.

I knew I'd have to face my sister today. I knew I couldn't stay in our little love bubble forever. But, God, I wanted to.

"I want to go home." I had to talk to my sister, tell her how sorry I was for worrying everyone again. I wished I could promise her that this would be the last time, but I knew I couldn't.

I was a recovering addict. It didn't matter how many times I promised them that I wouldn't relapse again, I could never be certain that it wouldn't happen. Yet I knew it was selfish and cowardly to go back to the high my body and mind craved – one I knew only ended in pain and regret, never mind the disappointment I caused my family, my friends, *Asher*.

He hadn't exactly said the words, but I saw the look on his face when he realized what I'd done after I'd left him the other day.

He didn't blame me, I knew that.

He wasn't angry. I knew that, too.

But he was disappointed in me, in the choice I made when I should have confided in him, trusted in him.

Looking up at his face, I saw a slack jaw and a relaxed demeanor. I waited for some reaction to what I said, but there was none.

Maybe he didn't hear me. Maybe he was wishing he hadn't heard those words. Maybe he didn't want me to go home.

Maybe he wanted me to stay.

"Ash?"

"No." I watched in trepidation as he opened his eyes and raised a hand, resting it against my cheek, gently taking hold of my chin, ensuring I couldn't look away from his intense, questioning gaze.

"I just got you back, Tayla. I'll take you to see your sister, if you want. But then you'll be coming right back here, with me. Where you *belong.*"

"Asher, I can't just—" I was rendered silent when, with a groan of annoyance, Asher sat up and dragged me into his lap. He framed my face in his hands, the urgency and desperation in the touch causing my heart to ache, my skin to sing from his touch.

"You're my world. I won't let you disappear on me again. I *can't.*"

"Baby..." The easily spoken endearment was dragged from my chest as the onslaught of emotions in Asher's eyes pulled me under, making me relive how it must have been for him when I left him, thinking I couldn't stay if he didn't want me anymore.

But it was just a misunderstanding, a lie I made myself believe in the wake of the hurt I felt and the mistrust I had in him.

I should have trusted him, all along.

"I'm here, Ash. I'm right here and I'm not going to disappear on you, on anyone, if I can help it."

I knew they weren't exactly the words he wanted to hear or the ones he needed in this moment. But I wouldn't let myself make promises I couldn't keep anymore.

I had to take control of my life again. I had to find a way to stay clean, with or without everything in my life going my way. Life wasn't always easy, but if I wanted a shot at a good, happy, healthy life, I had to try.

"I can't promise I won't get scared again, but I can promise that if I do, if I have doubts about us –"

"You come to me. You confide in me. No more walls, no more hiding and pretending that what we have isn't fuckin' *everything*." His voice had dropped to a near growl, the urgency and need for me in his tone sweeping me under, holding me captive.

I love him, so much. How could I have ever doubted that?

"I promise. *I love you.*"

Whoosh. I could barely get the words out before his hard, ardent mouth was covering mine, those big hands of his delving into my hair at both sides of my head while he hardened to life beneath me, his cock rubbing deliciously against my panties. My heart was in my throat as I gasped against his kiss, feeling his hands slide down to squeeze my bottom, his fingers digging into my flesh, telling me without words that I was his and only his.

And I was, I realized.

This man wasn't a bad boy or a player, like I'd thought when we first met. Maybe he had been in the past, but that wasn't the man who was here with me, now. He was good. So good, I wasn't sure I deserved him, if I were honest with myself.

He was protective to his core, with callus-ridden hands from the many nights he'd spent playing his guitar and scars all over from the time he'd spent in the Marines, a time he didn't talk about but I knew he would, one day. With me, I hoped.

Even though I'd opened myself up to him completely, that didn't mean he could trust me with his secrets, too. Maybe one day he would. I could tell there was something weighing on his mind, something he wasn't ready to tell me just yet.

Until then, until he felt like opening up fully, I would just love him and be there for him in any way I could, any way he allowed me to. I was completely and irrevocably his.

The only reason I would leave him now was if he asked me to.

"Asher, I need you. God, I need you so bad." I pled with him, the ache in my core undeniable, stronger than the shame of asking for my desires so blatantly, so openly.

Pulling my panties to the side with a sharp tug, Asher's eyes sparked with mischief and hunger, one I felt down to my core, too.

"*Mine.*" Hiking my ankles up on his shoulders, he dropped his head with a low groan of approval, no doubt seeing the embarrassing state of me, how *wet* I'd become for him just from the dry humping and that hot kiss he'd laid on me.

I had never been this hot and bothered over someone before.

He did that to me. Asher made me crazy with need and so happy, I was sure it was a dream at times.

As I felt the scrape of his stubble against my inner thighs, it was a reminder that this was real.

Dropping my head back, I moaned and whimpered as his hot, wet mouth never left my pussy. His tongue was licking and those lips of his I loved were sucking at me until I was sure I couldn't take it anymore.

"Ash! Please!"

"Come for me, baby. Come for me so I can do this again and again. I could eat you for fuckin' hours."

Just the mere idea of that pushed me over the edge, my body buzzing and aching in all the right places as I felt the high only Asher gave me and one I knew it was okay to be addicted to.

My eyes closed of their own accord as I melted into his chest, my face pressed tightly to his neck as my body hummed in the aftershocks of the most intense orgasm I'd ever had.

"You okay, Angel?"

"Mmm." Asher's hearty laugh met my ears as my eyes slid open, automatically finding his eyes filled with a warmth and love I wanted to look into again and again. Sex had always been a way to escape the pain for me. A way to get out of my head for a few minutes. But with him, it was different. It was *everything*, just like he'd said.

"Just rest now. I'll make us some breakfast, yeah?"

"Okay." Sleep started to take me as he got out of bed quietly, slipping on a pair of sweatpants and socks before leaving the room. Closing my eyes, I started to drift off but before I could, I heard him say something softly that I doubted he intended for me to hear.

"I'm sorry."

27

ASHER

"*I'm sorry.*" I whispered the words, though I knew my angel had dozed off into sleep after the orgasm I'd wrought from her. A reminiscent smile played across my face as I remembered the blissful grin she'd had on her face as she fell asleep, knowing her man would take care of her and that those worries and doubts and fears she'd had about us were laid to rest now.

I thanked God for that, but my guilt about letting her fall back into temptation, back into the claws of her addiction, was like a lead weight holding my chest, making it almost impossible to breathe around it.

How could I promise to protect her when I couldn't stop her from relapsing under my watch?

But, I didn't. My eyes sought out her pretty, sleeping face one more time before I made myself go into the kitchen and pull open the cabinet where I kept the pancake batter. I couldn't keep hiding this secret from her, I realized. I would make her some breakfast and then *tell her*.

I wasn't a man who liked keeping secrets. In my

experience, secrets only led to pain and anger when they were inevitably found out, or divulged. It was never going to be the right time to tell her that her little boy's mother was my sister. That the kind, loving couple she'd found for her child were closer to her life than she ever thought possible.

I should have told her before now. I knew that. God knows, I knew that. When she came back to me in pieces, thinking that somehow I didn't want her anymore, I should have come clean right then.

The reason I was on edge before she'd left wasn't because my feelings for her had changed. That wasn't possible. But the reality that the baby she'd lost was Spencer, my cute little nephew, was what had my head all kind of fucked-up.

The spoon in my hand felt heavy as I stirred the batter smooth, needing something to distract me from the conversation I had waiting for me when she woke up and saw the solemn look on my face.

I'd hoped she would have seen it in my eyes as I made love to her, kissing her with the desperation I felt, the idea of losing her one I couldn't stand – not when I had felt the panic and bone-chilling fear of discovering her gone, not knowing where she was or if she was okay.

"Fuck!" Gripping my head with both hands, I dropped the spoon into the bowl and paced the length of the kitchen, not knowing what was the right thing to do.

If I told her the truth, it would hurt her. How could she live with the knowledge that the son she gave up was so close, a nephew to the man she loved? Would she leave? *No.* Fuck, no. I wouldn't allow that to happen. I would tie her to my damn bed and force her to see that this didn't change anything between us.

Yes, it would be hard to see him, be near him. It could break my angel's spirit.

Could I do that to her?

Get a grip, Asher.

What would be the alternative? Letting her go?

"Ash?" Her sweet voice pulled me out of my head and my churning fears. Turning towards her, I gripped the counter behind me, my knees going weak at the thought of hurting her with what I had to tell her. She didn't deserve this. She deserved to be able to move on, petition the courts for custody of her son if she wanted to. She wouldn't even have that option now.

The woman I loved was a gentle spirit, a care-giver. She wouldn't do anything that could hurt another person. She would put my family over her own wants and needs and that was one of the many reasons I loved her.

But it wasn't fair to her. *None of this was fair.*

"You couldn't sleep?" The words felt like acid as they left my throat and the affection I usually felt for her was absent in the wake of my fear, my worry about what came next for us.

Tilting her head to one side, she rested herself against the exposed brick wall adjoining the kitchen and living room, her searching eyes on my face, wanting answers I was terrified to divulge.

But I would. I wasn't going to disappoint her and lie to her like those other men in her life. I promised her I would be there for her, no matter what happened. I meant that. I just wished it didn't mean hurting her in the process.

"Sit down, Tayla. I'll make you some coffee."

"You're worried." She didn't move from her spot, just regarded me with knowing eyes, as if she already knew about the secret that I had to tell her.

Sitting down at the table, I nodded, unwilling to lie to her anymore. She needed to know what she'd be risking by staying with me. The pain and heartbreak of losing her son, giving him up when he was just a newborn, would never be a distant memory for her. They'd always be there, at family gatherings, holidays, birthdays, even.

Sitting down in the chair next to me, she pressed her hand over mine and looked at me with such trust that it gave me the courage to open my mouth and *tell her*.

28

TAYLA

"*H*e's yours, Angel. I didn't know how to tell you. I tried to but never could get the words out."

"No," I whispered, unable to believe what I was hearing. It couldn't be true.

It just...couldn't.

"Angel, please listen to me." His words were full of desperation and fear, that bone-chilling, life-jarring fear you felt when you were in danger of losing someone close to you, maybe even someone you loved.

I wanted to relent, to believe that he would have told me, eventually.

The crisp edges of the picture I held in my hands made it obvious it was an old photo, but his face was as clear as day. My *son's* face stared back at me, the image of perfection in my eyes. His little upturned nose was scrunched up as if to complain about having his picture taken, his eyes were hazel, just like mine. His hands were raised up over his head as he played...

I wanted to be there in all of those little moments of his life. His first words, his first steps, the first time he called me mom. But the life I'd chosen before he came along didn't let me be there for him, or to be his mom, in any way that counted.

Yes, my blood, my DNA may have been running inside of him, but other than that, I would be a stranger to him now. Because I gave him up so he could have a better life. A happy one.

"This...this is your nephew?" It didn't make sense. I didn't want it to make sense. I felt as if I were in a state of shock, unable to comprehend how the sweet, adorable nephew Asher had told me about could be *my* son. *My* Spencer?

"I didn't know when we met, Tayla. I couldn't have. But, when you told me about your little boy and his name, I put it together." I watched him as he dropped his head into his hands and gripped angrily at his hair as if that would somehow fix this, make it go away, somehow.

When he finally looked back at me, I saw the look I'd wondered about last night. The dark, unreadable expression in his normally bright eyes that told of a secret, a lie, even.

God, I was so stupid, I realized. I'd thought he was keeping something from his past from me and was afraid to open up and scare me away.

But *this*? How could he have kept this from me?

"Why tell me now?" The words sounded harsh as I said them and a pang of regret filled my chest as I wished I could take them back. I knew Asher was a good man, an honest one. He'd proven that to me every day.

My eyes closed tightly as the pain in Asher's dark eyes became too much for me to face. The regret and guilt were clear as day in the way he looked at me, but it didn't matter. None of it mattered anymore, not even the love that still sang in my heavy chest for him. Because it was all a lie.

"I always planned on telling you, Angel. It just took me some time to wrap my head around it." *Right.* A part of me wanted to believe those words. Wanted to believe in the good, honest man I'd believed him to be.

But, this wasn't the first time lies and secrets had come from a man I thought was better than that. Trent had made me believe those things, too. And believing them, trusting him? It nearly broke me in the end.

It was hard to breathe against the weight of the truths he'd bared. My mind was warring against my heart as I tried to understand why he'd lied... why this was happening to us now.

I was finally happy, in love with a man who protected me, cared for me, loved me with his whole heart.

I should have known it was too good to be true.

Good things never lasted for me. Why would he be any different?

Shaking my head, I wiped roughly at my cheeks, my skin burning from the tears that slid down my face in the wake of the truth, one I couldn't wrap my head around just yet.

"I... I need time." The words seemed so hauntingly shallow compared to the gravity of the emotion that welled up inside me... emotion that shook me to my core, while that very part of me longed for it to be false, a lie or some sick, sad joke my head was playing on me – anything to make the words rattling around in my head on an endless loop less true, less real.

My heart stopped as Asher's sad, pain-filled eyes met mine, eyes that looked like a gray rain-cloud as the storm of his emotions, just like mine, overtook him. And we just stood there, too broken, too lost to move, to break away as our eyes locked for a moment that felt like an eternity, but in reality only lasted a few measly minutes.

"Tay..."

"No, I can't...I don't..."

The words I wanted to say were right there on the tip of my tongue, wanting to slip free. They were words of understanding, words of forgiveness and kindness – the very things Asher had given me as I'd pushed him away, disappearing on him whenever we got too close and, inevitably, when I relapsed, not so long ago.

But my heart couldn't do it, couldn't let go of the pain and the anger and confusion his confession had caused. He hadn't just kept something from me, he'd kept my baby boy from me.

If I'd known, I wasn't sure if I would have done anything about it, but I would have had that choice. For so long, I'd let people around me make my choices for me. I wouldn't go back to that. *I couldn't.*

"Just...let me go, Ash."

And with those whispered, anguished words, I stumbled back to his bedroom, finding my bag and my clothes, making sure I had everything I needed before I left him.

I wasn't sure for how long. I wasn't sure if it would be a *just for now* distance between us, or *forever*.

All I knew was that if I didn't go now, I wasn't sure I'd have the strength to, once I let myself break in the wake of the sadness and uncertainty that swarmed my heart and battered my soul.

I just had to get out of there, away from the source of my pain.

And right then? That source was Asher.

29

ASHER

"*I* fucked up." Understatement of the fucking century, but it was the only way I knew how to describe the colossal way I'd broken things with Tayla. *My* Tayla.

Would she really be mine after the storm broke? After she let herself realize the extent of the lie I'd told her? And why?

I'd been afraid of hurting her, causing any more pain and regret for the choices she'd made in the darkest time in her young life. No woman – scratch that, no *one* – should have to weather the kind of hurricane of pain and heartache that this girl had. And somehow, she'd done it without losing sight of the beautiful, sassy, kind, loving person she had been before her addiction, before losing her son, before everything bad in her world had hit her like a damn freight train.

More than anything, I'd been afraid that making her face up to the possibility of getting her son back would be the last straw for her, the one thing that would break her resolve to be clean and sober again.

What if I'd told her and she'd relapsed, pushed me away for good?

How could I have fuckin' lived with myself?

I should have taken the chance, I realized.

She wasn't some damsel in distress. I wasn't her keeper, I didn't have the right to keep secrets from her, especially one that could have given her boy back.

"Asher? Are you there?" Blake's concern-etched voice pulled me from my thoughts, brought me back to why I'd called him in the first place. Normally when I felt like this – uneasy and confused, angry and scared out of my motherfuckin' mind – I went to Ben, my big brother and the one person in my life who always gave it to me straight, no bullshit.

Oftentimes, I needed that harsh dose of reality, of real, blunt truth.

But this time, I needed something different. I knew I'd made the royal mistake of keeping the truth from my sweet, beautiful girl, my angel. *My* Tayla.

Blake knew her better than most. He was her confidant, her safe place to run to when it felt like the world was tumbling down all around her, when her fear of relapse was too great, that crippling fear that held her captive most days. But she was strong, the strongest person I knew.

She could rise above all that pain and sadness and fear, all of the things that had kept her grounded for so long. She was better now. She was healing from the abuse her ex brought to her life, the self-hatred and heart-breaking sorrow that had led her down the path of addiction, that held her captive, under lock and key. She was a fighter and if I had it my way, I would stand by her side as she fought each and every one of those demons, sword in hand, my heart in her hands.

A loud knock on the front door of my apartment had my thoughts halting, though they never really strayed from Tayla. Never far from her, that was for damn sure. Knowing Blake, he had headed over here when he'd heard my panicked voice on the phone, only minutes after I'd realized Tayla hadn't just wanted space, she'd wanted space from *me*.

This morning already felt like weeks ago, us in bed together with nothing but my high thread count sheets separating us. Now, it felt like the world was separating us, the secret I'd let slither its way into our lives causing the distance between us now.

I pulled the door of my apartment open with trepidation, unsure if I was going to be met with a punch to the face for hurting his sister, or with a look of pity when he saw the sad state I was in after I'd done just that. Intentional or not, I'd lied to her, keeping her from the truth because I'd just been too afraid of losing her, losing the woman I loved more than anything in this whole goddamn world.

Selfish? Yeah, I had been. But hurting her was never something I wanted to do. And by the time I'd realized what I had done, it was too late to change a damn thing.

"Shit, you look like shit, man."

Forcing myself to crack a smile at his jab, I shrugged my shoulders as if to say, *I feel like shit, too*.

And the only person in my life who could change that was the one who wanted absolutely nothing to do with me.

My fault, I reminded myself. I could feel bad for myself all I wanted, but it didn't change the fact that I needed to figure out a way to fix all of this, if that were even possible. My girl was honest, down to her core. She'd made enough mistakes in her past to know that secrets were pointless, especially keeping one from someone you loved.

I felt the same way.

So why hadn't I fucking told her the truth?

"Thanks a lot. You want a beer?" I opened my fridge and pulled out two just in case, while Blake roamed around my apartment, as if this were the perfect opportunity for a fucking tour. Though I should have counted myself lucky that he'd come at all. Tayla was his sister, after all. And I knew from my many talks with him about her to know that he was just as fiercely protective over her as I was with Ally.

The fact that he was willing to be there for me, as a friend, was a big step in the right direction. If anyone could get through to Tayla right now, I was pretty sure it would be him.

"She texted me." *Fuck.* Opening my beer, I took a long, slow swig of it before handing him the other one.

"How is she?" There were a hundred different questions I wanted to ask, but that one seemed to be the only one that mattered. That and *where is she?*

I knew she wasn't happy with me and I knew I couldn't take back the secret I'd kept from her, but I just wanted her home. If she wanted me to sleep on the couch, I would. If she wanted to yell at me, scream and hit me for being so completely stupid, I'd happily let her. I just wanted her here, in my home, one I knew she thought of as her own even though she'd only been here a handful of times.

We could fix us. I had to believe that.

"She asked me to check on you. And to tell you

that she'll talk when she's ready." Closing my eyes, I let myself feel a tiny glimmer of hope that she hadn't completely written me off just yet. She'd been hurt, yes, but the love she felt for me was real. *We* were real. If she wanted her brother to check on me and make sure I was okay, that had to be a good sign, right?

"I'm gonna get her back, Blake. Make this right. And I need your help."

"If you hurt her again, I won't be so quick to help you. You know that, right?" His eyes met mine with all the brotherly love and protectiveness I'd come to expect from him and, nodding solemnly, I knew this was my one chance to make things right between us.

With her brother's help, I felt like I had a fighting chance.

"I have no intention of ever hurting her again as long as I fuckin' live. I just want to get her back so we can fix what I've managed to break."

Speaking with all of the emotion I could muster, I let my love for Tayla show in my face so he knew just how deeply I needed to make things right with her before it was too late.

Before she pushed me away for good.

"Alright, what's the plan?"

30

ASHER

*H*er eyes were wide as fuckin' saucers as I stood up from my seat at the very back of the dining hall where her Narcotics Anonymous meetings were always held. I knew, because I'd followed her here a few times. I couldn't help it. I wanted to always be around her, always have her sweet scent around me, her face in my view. She'd invited me once, after her relapse and having her trust me enough to have me here meant more than I knew she'd ever realize.

After Blake had agreed to help, he received a text from Scarlet saying that she was dragging my beautiful girl to a meeting, saying she wasn't happy about it but that it was what she needed. I was sure her spirits were crushed after hearing the truth last night and, though a part of me knew she'd asked for space, I also knew that she needed me now, more than ever. I had to do something to make things right between us again. This was as good a start as any because, whether we were together or not, I wanted her to be healthy and happy and sober.

I wanted her to have the life she'd dreamed about

before her ex tainted those dreams, that carefree spirit I knew she once had. And if showing up to her meeting uninvited did that, I'd deal with her being mad at me. Because it was worth ensuring her happiness.

"Ash..." She whispered her nickname for me, one that had my heart racing, just as it always did.

"No, just listen, alright?" Pushing through the aisle on my way to her, I muttered a few apologies as a few of her peers grumbled at my rudeness. But right then? I didn't care. I just needed to get to her. Now.

"I know you're used to doing everything on your own – being alone in anything and everything you need to do – but Tayla, I'm here. I'm here for fuckin' everything. I don't want to go through this life without *you*. I don't want to fall asleep without *you*. I don't want to even think about anything without you right next to me."

Grabbing one of her hands in both of mine, I let my weak knees send me to her feet, only moving to find the ring Blake and Ally had helped me find at a local jewelry store today. After telling my sister how I had omitted the truth, about who Tayla was and what she meant to me, she knew my girl deserved a place in her little boy's life.

I'm not sure what that will mean, but I do know this. This woman is my anchor, my lifeline and my fucking world. We could figure everything else out.

If only she'd say yes.

Tears shone in my girl's eyes as she let our fingers entwine, softening to me for the first time since the truth of her son had come out between us. A sliver of hope filled my chest; the knowledge that she hadn't completely written me off warming me up from the inside, out.

"You shouldn't have kept it from me."

"I know." *Fuck.* I knew that to be true. If I could go back, I would change my lie, my cowardly actions. But I couldn't do that. All I could do was resolve to spend the rest of my life making her forget I ever chose to keep something so huge from her, and making her happier than she could imagine being.

"I thought I could cushion the blow somehow. Find a better, less painful way to tell you. It was my stupid, fucked-up way of protecting you, Angel."

Her lips twitched at the term of endearment I always used for her and her face split into a small smile as she squeezed my hand as if to say, *I love you.*

Could she still love me after what I'd done?

Jesus, I hoped so.

"It's not stupid. I love that you want to protect me, Ash. It's who you are and I promise, I don't want to change that. It's actually one of my favorite things about you. Your heart is so big, so loving and it's what made me fall in love with you so quickly. It was hard not to love you."

I could see in her eyes that she meant every word. Tracing her fingers with my thumbs, I wondered if this was fate, somehow. That the universe had somehow put us on this course and everything we'd both been through — every up, every down — just meant that we were finally ready to give each other the love we both deserved.

"But, omitting the truth in order to protect me isn't what I want. Please, Ash, I need *you* to be the one to tell me the truth, even if it will hurt me. Because even if it does, I'll have your love to get me through."

"I will never keep anything from you again, Angel. On one condition."

My heart was hammering as she frowned and finally looked down at my knees, pressed to the hardwooden floorboards, and the small Zale's box clutched in one of my hands.

"Oh, my God, *Asher.*"

"Yeah, baby this is happening." Lifting myself up on one of my knees, which ached from the hardness of the floor beneath me, I pulled one of her dainty hands to my mouth and pressed a kiss to her ring finger, right where my ring would be for the rest of her life, if I had any say in the matter.

"You're under my skin, Angel. You're all I want in this life and the next and every one after. If there is an afterlife for me after I leave you, I want you in that one, too. I swear on everything that matters to me that I will *never* lie to you again. Not for the rest of our lives."

A tearful but happy sob-laugh came from her as she nodded her head at my promise, making the question lingering on the very tip of my tongue that much easier to divulge.

"Tayla Marie Reynolds, will you *marry* me?"

Wiping at her overflowing tears, the sight of which broke my heart, she just laughed that sweet, happy laugh I loved so much and nodded.

"Stupid question, Ash."

"I still need an answer," I begged her. I knew from her reaction that it was a given that she'd marry me but, for some reason, I needed to hear those words from her delectable lips.

Sinking onto her knees in front of me, her hands encompassed my face, her thumb tracing my lips the way she often did when she was feeling shy. Pulling her in with my arms around her waist, I pinched her sides playfully, earning myself a smack to my chest before she met my eyes and smiled so sweetly, I felt sure I would have fallen to my knees if I hadn't already done just that.

"Words, baby. Now." I had never been a man who was capable of begging a woman for anything, but that's what she'd turned me into. But only for *her*.

"Yes, my big, silly man. I will marry you."

God, how I'd craved to hear those words.

Smiling so widely my face hurt, I crushed her to my chest and buried my nose in her hair, inhaling her scent into my lungs and embedding the memory of this into my mind, forever.

I wasn't *ever* letting her go.

31

ASHER

6 MONTHS LATER

"*Y*ou ready, Angel?" Turning into the cul-de-sac of my sister's home, I knew the answer to my question without even looking at my wife.

Wife. Jesus, I still couldn't believe she'd agreed to marry me. I was a lucky son of a bitch.

"What if he doesn't—" Hearing her words break with the uncertainty I knew she was feeling broke my heart. Looking down at her lap, she refused to look at me and I just wouldn't have that. There was no more hiding with us, we were long past that.

"He will." Grabbing one of her hands in mine, I cupped her smooth cheek with my other, waiting until those gorgeous eyes of hers landed on me.

"He knows about you and he knows you're his real mom, the one that brought him into this world. If Ally says he's ready, then we have to believe he is."

Nodding her head, she smiles softly, leaning her head into my hand as I stroked her cheek, knowing that sometimes she just needed a reminder that she wasn't alone anymore— she never would be, again.

From now on, she would always have me by her side, her protector, her best friend, her husband for the rest of our damn lives.

She would *never* have to be alone and afraid, again.

Her eyes shone with unshed tears as she looked at me, the trust in those eyes of hers made me feel like her fuckin' hero. *God,* I loved her.

"Ready?" I probed again, fully intending on staying right here, reassuring her until she was.

Pushing her to see her son before she was ready wasn't something I would do. But knowing how much she'd missed him, day in and day out for the past three years told me that she wanted this more than she'd say and that was what drove me to push the issue with my sister, making her see that having Tayla in her son's life would be a blessing, just another person for their baby boy to love.

With another nod, she opens her door, reaches for her purse on the floor and gives me another soft, beautiful—as—hell smile before she closes the door and meets me at the front of my truck, her hand instantly searching out mine, her eyes going to the front door of the house as we walk up the stairs, hand in hand.

Knocking on the door, I lower my head to trail my lips over the top of her head, smiling when she leans into me like she always does. It may have taken us longer than most to get here, together and happy, but I wouldn't have changed a thing about our love story. It's ours. It's real. It's us.

"Oh! You're here." Ally answers the door with a wide, happy smile, her hair in a big, messy bun and her feet in those fluffy slippers she always wears. Shaking my head at her, I pull her into my chest for a hug, keeping Tayla's hand securely in mine, just to remind her that I'm right here, with her.

"Missed your annoying little sister?"

"Of course, I did. Is he awake?" Peering into the house, I spot little feet behind her, running up to hide behind her legs, eyes identical to the woman I loved peeking out from between them.

"Say hi, little man. Your mama Tayla came to see you." His eyes got wide as he looked up at his mom, almost as if he was waiting for her to tell him she was kidding, that his real mom wasn't really there to see him.

He'd seen pictures of Tayla as he'd grown up and even face-timed her over the past few months, talking to her on the phone every night until Ally and Charlie were convinced, he was ready to see her, have her in his life without confusion or fear.

"There's my baby boy." Releasing my hand, Tayla drops down to her knees so she's on Spencer's level and as she reaches out a hand to him, she looks up at me, such strength and love in her eyes for the son I know she'd wished for, longed for.

And here he was, just a few inches away from her reach.

32

TAYLA

"There's my baby boy." My stomach turned with longing, a deep-seated, long ignored need to hold the little boy in front of me, just one more time. *He's so big.* I couldn't help the feeling that I'd missed *everything* with my baby. He was two, now. Walking and talking and laughing, now. How could I have ever thought I was better off without him a part of my life?

But that wasn't the case, was it? It was him who'd been better without me around him, a constant sense of trouble and worry as he grew up, always knowing he hadn't been enough to keep my demons at bay. Would I have tried to get clean, sober and healthy for him? Of course.

But without rehab and my meetings, without Asher and Blake and Scar in my life, would I have been strong enough to make it last? To be the mother this beautiful boy deserved?

Everything happens for a reason. The sentiment I'd often told myself when my world seemed dark and without purpose whispered through my mind and now I knew why I'd had to go through everything I had— it was for him. I would do it all over again just to be his mom, be the mom he would need, one he could be proud of.

Reaching out my hand to him, I let my eyes look up into Asher's— the unconditional and always present love I saw there giving me the reassurance I needed, without having to ask for it.

Because he knew me, he always had. He could feel what I needed before I ever had the chance to ask for it and that was just one of the million other reasons I loved and needed him in my life, *forever*.

"Are you my real mom?" The whispered question was one I would never forget as I moved my gaze from my husband to my son and nodding my head, I let my tears of relief fall against my cheeks. I curled my fingers around his tiny ones, his soft skin under my fingertips reminded me of the first time I'd held him in my arms, counting all his little toes and his little fingers as I reveled in the reality that this angel was my son, even if I'd thought I would never see him, again.

Every day since then, I'd fought the darkness shrouding my life and pushed myself toward the life I knew was waiting for me on the other side of it, if I could just keep going, keep fighting to get back to him. Looking down at my son, now, I realized, I had.

This moment was real and no matter what happened tomorrow, next year or ten years from now, no one could take this day away from us.

"Yes, baby. Do you remember me?" Tipping his head to the side, he let go of Aly's leg and wrapped his hand around my cheek as he nodded in the cutest way.

"I think so. My mommy's told me that you were sad and needed to find your happy before you could come for me." If that wasn't the best way to describe recovery to a small child, I wasn't sure what was.

"Yes, they were right." Pulling him into my arms, a soft sob broke free from my chest as his little hands curled around my neck as if he'd missed me just as much as I'd missed him.

"I missed you, my baby boy," I whispered into his chubby neck and he just held me tighter, as if to say *I love you*.

I felt Asher's warm, strong arms come around the both of us and I knew this is what I'd been fighting for all this time.

It was my son. It was my husband. It was this family that brought me into their lives so easily, loving me as if I was their own. It was my happiness, my home.

My *forever*.

EPILOGUE

FIVE YEARS LATER

"*I*t's perfect, Angel." Hanging the last ornament on a branch towards the top of the tree, I grinned— not at all surprised that my wife had waited until an hour before the party to decorate the huge, evergreen tree that filled the living room, now. I watched her as she rocked back on the heels of her Christmas shoes, as she loved to call them. They were a pair of high heeled, cowboy boots that I had gotten her our first Christmas together and over the years, she'd added ribbons to the laces for each Christmas, since. They were a tribute to our love, our family and reminded me how *motherfuckin'* lucky I was to call the beauty before me, mine.

"*Yeah*? The popcorn isn't too much?" She scrunched her nose up in that adorable way she always does and shaking my head at her, I draw her close to my chest before dropping my nose to nuzzle her neck, breathing her in; reminding myself of the blessing that was my angel; my life.

"Nat and Ben should be here, soon. Do you want to go get the kids ready for pictures?" Her mouth rested against my ear as she spoke, causing my cock to come to life from behind the jeans I wore; not much of a surprise when it came to her.

"Yeah, baby. You go get that pretty dress on before I fuckin' take you, right here. You'd like that wouldn't you, my angel?" Letting my hands roam to her ass, I took my time in exploring her skin before wrapping my fingers around her plump flesh and squeezing in a reminder of just who she belonged to. *Always would belong to.*

My angel married me on Christmas day, five years ago and though we always spent the night before with her big, Italian family, tomorrow would be ours.

All ours.

I'd already made sure that my parents would be picking up Spencer and Alice so I would have my wife, all to myself. I was a greedy and jealous bastard when it came to her and I didn't care if that made me a bad man. Because when it came to her, I was lost- completely and utterly lost and I wouldn't have it any other way. If the way Tayla looked at me through her lashes as she dashed up the stairs to our bedroom was any indication, she felt the same-fuckin'-way.

"Stop ogling your wife and help us with these fuckin' gifts, brother." An amused laugh left me at the sound of Ben's grumbling voice, not at all surprised that he was annoyed, already. He was supposed to here ten minutes ago, but as I walked to the front door and watched his redheaded bombshell of a wife get out of the driver's side of their Jeep, I knew exactly why they'd been late.

I loved the woman like a damn sister but she couldn't be on time to save her life. I'd told him this when they'd first started dating, but he was so far gone over her, he was doomed from the very start. And now we didn't even blink an eye when he arrived late for every damn family dinner or holiday get together. It was basically tradition, now.

"Did you buy the whole damn toy store, Nat?" I teased her as I met her by the trunk door, wrapping her in a tight hug before pulling back and cracking a smile I knew she'd melt over. As she always did.

"It's Alice's birthday in a few days, isn't it? Two birds, one stone, right?" With a shrug of her shoulders, she passed me a box of gifts before knocking her hip into mine before leading the way to the house.

At the reminder of my baby girl's birthday, I realized I'd been so ensnared in preparing for our anniversary that I'd completely forgotten about the other big day we had coming up.

And I felt like a fuckin' ass, forgetting my own baby's birthday.

"Yo, Ben! Get your ass in my car. We've got to go on an errand." I hollered into the house, hoping to God that my angel didn't hear the panic in my voice, or rather didn't hear me at all.

I wasn't the forgetful type. And I wasn't an absentee father. My own dad had taught me much better than that. But between helping Lucas with his album, managing the office at the studio while Ben took vacation this past week and juggling my other artists, I was wearing myself thin.

It wasn't an excuse, though. I didn't care if it was Christmas eve. And I didn't care if we had to drive to fuckin' Montana to find the Barbie Jeep my baby girl had been hinting at since Thanksgiving, I'd find it and bring it home for her because she was worth it.

That girl was my whole damn world.

We hadn't had it easy when we'd finally decided we wanted to try for a baby of our own. While Spencer would always be my little man, spending every other weekend with us and whenever else we could steal him away, from the moment I'd met my angel, I'd imagined her round with *my* baby. Getting pregnant wasn't easy for us at first and our beautiful Alice had come at a time when we were sure a baby wasn't in the cards for us. She was a miracle that came at the exact right time and though I'd almost lost my angel during her birth, I was damn thankful she'd come into our lives.

Our little family was complete when she came into the world and it didn't matter how many times Tayla asked me what I wanted for Christmas- I meant it when I said that I had everything I needed in our little family.

It was more than I'd ever deserved but I was a selfish man and took it, anyways.

❧

"Stop beating yourself up, brother." Lucas grumbled from the back of the Jeep as we drove toward the heart of downtown, where the biggest toy store in town was somehow still open. Rocking my head in my hands, I didn't know how my brothers could be so chill about the fact that I'd forgotten my own fuckin' daughter's birthday. My baby girl was such a good, sweet girl in every way and the thought of her pretty eyes watering because I forgot her big day was like a punch straight to my fuckin' chest.

"How could I have forgotten, Luke? She's my *baby*."

"You don't think Dad forgot one of our birthdays growing up? He was on tour half the time and the other half he was working odd jobs around town. You've got a lot on your plate, man. And even if you can't get her that Jeep, she'll still love the shit out of you 'cus you're her dad."

Despite the fact that we often thought of Luke as our goofy, baby brother, his advice had a ring of truth to it. That didn't stop me from feeling like shit about it, though.

"Yeah. I know. Thanks, brother." Feeling him squeeze my shoulder from the back seat, I sat back and sighed. I couldn't wait to get home and hug my two favorite girls.

The long days at the studio and the stress from the holidays were all fuckin' worth it when I remembered what I had waiting for me, each and every night.

I was a lucky man, that was for damn sure.

"Alright, let's do this." Ben rumbled as soon as he rolled into a parking spot closest to the entrance of *Moe's Toys and Tricks*. I grinned to myself, remembering how our mom brought us here as kids to pick out a toy or two. And after she was gone, Dad had picked up the tradition, bringing us here after each of our little league games until we grew out of the thrill of coming here. It was small moments like this that her memory would hit me and though I was happy my Dad had found love again in Elsa, there wasn't a holiday that passed that I didn't wish for just one more day with my mom. Sniffing away the sudden sting of tears behind my eyes, I followed my brothers into the store and tried to shake off the sudden reminiscent thoughts plaguing my mind.

"You okay, man?" Ben's hand settled on my back as we ventured towards the Barbie section of the store and I nodded, giving a shrug of my shoulders as if to say *It's fine*. Because though I missed mom every damn day, I'd become a pro at hiding it. Grief like this didn't just fade over time. It changed with time, became more natural to remember her without the crippling pain that came with knowing we'd never see her smile or hear her laugh, again.

"Shit, we got lucky." Luke rounded the corner of the aisle and grinned, holding up a pink, sparkly, Barbie Jeep in one of his hands before heaving it into the shopping cart he'd snagged from the front of the store.

Maybe Mom had been looking out for her grandbaby, sending a bit of look our way.

Smiling at the thought, my eyes snagged on a few new Barbie collections at the end of the aisle and I threw those in, too, wanting to see my girl smiling from ear to ear when she opened them up.

"Come on, let's get out of here. Kaelyn already texted asking where I disappeared to." Luke said with a laugh, and rolling my eyes I pushed the cart toward a self checkout lane, knowing I'd hear them bickering as soon as we got back to the house.

I loved my brother something fierce but his wife had to have patience to deal with his annoying ass all the time. I'd gotten used to them arguing over silly shit he'd do all the time and eventually, it was just background noise to us. At our knowing looks, he threw his blonde head back on a laugh.

"I like riling her up, that's the point."

If anything, Christmas would be entertaining if he had anything to do with it.

~

Pulling up to the house, I climbed out first, spotting my two favorite girls building a snow man in the front yard. As soon as she saw me, Alice squealed and took off toward me, her mittens still filled with snow. But as she wrapped her arms around my legs and hugged me, I didn't mind one bit. Picking her up under her arms and spinning her around as I always did, I planted her on my hip and walked over to my angel as she pushed a carrot nose into the snow man they'd built, her nose scrunching up in concentration and making me hard in a matter of seconds.

This girl could do anything and I'd be hard. God, *I fuckin' loved her.*

"Why don't you go on in and warm up, baby. We'll be right in." Letting Alice down, I bent down to kiss her hair, ruffling it until she giggled and pushed me away, running into the house and taking off her shoes at the door. *Good girl.*

"Where did you run off to?"

The guilt came right back as her bright, hazel eyes peered up at me, her fingers toying with my hair that I'd let grow well past my neck over the past few months.

"Oh, Ash." Her gaze softened and her nose scrunched up as she pushed her chest into mine, encircling my shoulders with her arms in a tight hold I didn't know I needed until that very moment.

"I'm sorry, Angel. There's no fuckin' excuse-"Pulling back from my hold on her, she just shook her head, some emotion pulling at her face as she looked up at me like I was her whole world.

There was no question that she was mine.

"Do you remember Spencer's birthday last year? When you found me wrapping presents late that night?" Her question came out of the blue and rocking my head back, I thought back to that night when she'd insisted on waiting to wrap our boy's presents until after everyone had gone to sleep. I just laughed it off, knowing my girl was many things and procrastinator was obviously one of them. I hadn't thought any more about it until now.

"Yeah, I do. You were wrapping them in the dark, silly girl."

"I didn't want him to wake up and realize that while he'd been counting up the days 'till his birthday, I'd somehow forgotten it was coming up. It took Natalie to remind me the day before and the guilt almost crushed me once I realized I'd almost forgotten my baby boy's big day."

Fuck. My angel was perfect in my eyes; in every way. Watching her grow into her maternal instincts was fuckin' beautiful and not once; not ever did I doubt her love for both our children.

But she was human. She had a lot on her plate, just like I did and often I forgot that. I wanted to be the best man for her, the best father to our kids and the best damn husband she could have dreamed up in that pretty head of hers.

But that didn't mean I'd be perfect- that was impossible as much as I wished to be everything my girls needed in this life and any life after this.

"I never would have guessed, Angel. You're the best fuckin' mom." I gritted the words roughly, securing my hand around the back her neck while my thumb sought out her chin, drawing it up until her eyes were back on mine.

The soft blush that covered her face revealed that my tone had turned her on but the love- pure and unwavering love that shone from her eyes told me she didn't blame me for one second, loving me despite my carelessness.

"You're the best dad to that girl in there, Ash. *Please* tell me you believe that."

Even if I hadn't believed her words, I would have lied right then. Because the trust and love she bathed me in was like a balm to my once dark soul.

After my time overseas, watching one too many of my friends die right before my damn eyes had done a number on my view of the world; a world that was dark and filled with pain I felt first hand. But meeting my angel had changed all of that. Loving her taught me that I needed light to make my way out of the dark place I'd found myself in before finding her.

She was my light.

"Yeah, baby, I do." Pulling her in by her luscious hips, I took her mouth in a soft kiss knowing it was more than likely that one or both my brothers would be watching from the house.

I'd always been the single one, the player, the bad boy of the three of us.

Now that I had settled down and had my angel to curb my player ways, my brothers rarely missed a chance to hassle me about it. *Fuckers.*

"*Get inside.*" I muttered on a groan of annoyance, knowing that I wouldn't get the chance to sample my wife until everyone went home which wouldn't be 'till much later tonight.

I would have to suffer through dinner with this raging, unrelenting hard on and I would gladly suffer for this girl. But she *would* be paying for it, later.

"Tonight, you're mine, Angel." Growling the words in her ear, I forced myself to pull back from her warmth, settling for intertwining our hands as I led her back to the house where everyone was gathered inside, the sound of Christmas music hitting my ears as we stepped inside.

Tayla's hand squeezed mine as I lifted my baby girl into my arms, kissing her cheek before I let my eyes drift back to my wife; they never strayed from her for long.

Leaning in to whisper into my ear like the vixen she was, my erection became painful as her teasing words filled my head.

"You better make good on that promise, Husband."

And hell, if I didn't want to bend her right then, no matter the consequences.

Christmas be damned.

But, given the knowledge that this was her favorite holiday, I just kissed her long and hard only pulling away when I was sure she'd lost every naughty thought in her head.

"I love you, *dirty girl.*" The words weren't needed, because she felt my love for her every second, every damn day. I said them anyway. As I would for the rest of our fuckin' lives.

～

"Do you really have to go, Uncle Ben?"

"Unfortunately, you're mean Auntie says we do." I had to bite back a laugh as I watched my youngest niece wrap her little arms around Ben's legs, as if that would surely stop him from leaving the party early.

After I'd hidden Alice's gifts in the upstairs closet along with the rest of what we'd gotten our two little terrors, we'd had a big, family dinner with both my parents and Tayla's, Blake and his girlfriend, Lacey stopped by, too.

He was a self-proclaimed bad boy, but just as I'd been lost in love after meeting my angel, he was gone over his girl quickly after meeting her. Watching him dote over her during dinner told me what Tayla had already seen for herself; her brother was in love.

Poor fucker.

My niece was still peering up at my brother with big, puppy dog eyes as my angel walked back into the room, a dish rag in her hands and *my smile* spreading that delectable mouth of hers.

I'd put that mouth to good use, later.

"Hey, Angel. All cleaned up?" The warmth of her hand slipping into mine spread up my arm and right to my damn chest as I pulled her in close, dropping my nose to the base of her neck to breathe her in as I always did when I had her this close.

"Scarlet helped me. You're doing it next year, though." The tease in her tone dripped from the words but I still smiled the crooked, cocky smile I knew melted her, every time.

"We'll see about that, Angel."

"But I haven't even opened my present yet!" Little Heather's pleading voice had me pulling partially away from Tayla's hold on me, unable to help the low laugh that left me when she turned her puppy dog eyes on me, as if I could deny her a damn thing.

This girl had all of us wrapped around her little finger and she *knew* it.

"We'll be here bright and early for breakfast and

presents, Pumpkin." Ben said as he knelt down so he was on her level, ruffling her blonde hair- just like her mama's.

Her big, green eyes twinkled with excitement then and nodding her head, she rushed past us into the living room where she'd already spotted the gift she wanted to open, tonight.

It was of-course, the biggest one under the tree.

"I'll see y'all tomorrow. If I get home in one piece with this one driving." He was teasing his wife as he said the words, but when she turned her icy blue eyes on him, there was no mistake the tension that shook him.

She was the sweetest woman on the outside but inside she had sass in her that no one wanted heading their way. My brother had his work cut out for him with her, but I knew he didn't mind one bit. He was as love drunk as I was.

"Drive safe, Nat. Try not to kill my brother, yeah?" Hugging her close, I clapped my brother on the back as I closed the front door behind them on a shake of my head.

"Poor guy," My angel whispers the words in my ear as she nibbles on my earlobe, her hands drifting down my back to where I need them most.

"Easy, baby. Let's put the kids down and then, I'm all yours." Squeezing her ass in my hands, I kissed her soft and slow, letting her know with my mouth just how I was going to fuck her, later.

Nice and slow and rough. *Just how she liked it.*

∼

"Mama," Rolling to my side in bed, I peered an eye open to see Alice standing in the partially opened doorway, rubbing at her sleepy eyes with her hands.

"Baby, what's wrong?" Sitting up, I pulled a tired hand over my head, worry for my baby girl at the forefront of my mind. It had to be well past midnight by now. She was normally a heavy sleeper, almost always sleeping through the night without question.

Maybe she'd had a nightmare. *My poor girl.*

"Come here, baby. Did you have a bad dream?" Pulling her into my lap, I wrapped an arm around her tightly, letting my fingers sift through her auburn hair in hopes of calming her down enough to sleep. She hadn't had to sleep in our bed for a while, but I didn't mind it, tonight.

It was her birthday, after all.

"I think so. I woke up scared." Wrapping her little hands around my neck, she snuggled in tight, fitting perfectly in my arms; as she always had. When she was born, she was tiny and I was often afraid of dropping her she was so fragile, so sweet. And though she'd grown in strides since then, she was still my little girl. *And she always would be.*

While I loved Tayla in a consuming, obsessive, sometimes irrational way, I would do anything for this girl right here. If anything threatened to touch a hair on her fuckin' head, I wouldn't hesitate to protect her with my damn life. *Not even for a second.*

Her sniffle against my chest had my protective instincts surging, even while I knew there wasn't a real thing she was afraid of, it was just a bad dream.

"Shh, it's okay, baby girl. Daddy's got you. I'll always have you."

Lifting her head from my neck, she hits me with a

wide, sweet smile and my chest filled with pride, love and purpose that only being a dad could give me.

"I love you, Daddy." Smiling against her hair, I whispered the words back to her but had to pull back when the shrill sound of my cell phone ringing beside the bed interrupted the moment.

"Hang on, baby. Lay down with mommy for a minute." Laying her down on Tayla's side, I kissed her cheek before begrudgingly climbed out of bed, sitting on the edge as I picked up my phone; confusion filling my gut as I saw my father's name across the screen.

"Dad, everything okay?" The silence on the other side of the phone had dread like nothing I'd felt before seeping through my chest and spreading the longer he didn't answer me.

"*Dad?*" Though I knew my girls were safe and sound behind me, I couldn't help the fear that went through me at the thought of something happening to them. A call in the middle in the night couldn't be good, *right?*

"It's Ben, son. He needs us." *Fuck!*

"What—where is he?" I was having trouble getting my thoughts together as my chest tightened and my hands begun to shake.

He may have been my goofy older brother, but he was also my best *fuckin'* friend.

I couldn't lose him. I couldn't lose someone else.

"Baby? What's going on?" Feeling my angel's warm fingers on my nape, I leant my back into her chest as her arms wrapped my waist, as if even in her dreams she'd known her man needed her.

God, did I need her, now.

"St. James Hospital. Nat...*Fuck,* we don't know if

she's waking up." *Nat.* Only then did I remember that Natalie had been driving so if they'd crashed...

"Fuck. I'm coming, Dad."

"Alright, son. See you soon." Hanging up the phone, I looked down at the blank screen for way longer than needed, just because I couldn't believe this was happening.

It was Christmas for fucks sake.

Fuck you, fate. Turning my head to meet Tayla's worried, sleepy gaze, I wished I didn't have to say the words that slipped past my suddenly dry lips.

"There's been an accident."

Thank you so much for taking the time to read *Saving Tayla*. This novel especially was incredibly hard for me to write, as you may know if you follow me online. It contains triggers for me and for I'm sure some of my readers, as well. If you loved this story as much I did, please feel free to leave a review. And if you haven't followed me, my links are below.

Love,
Amanda

PLAYLIST

Anxiety by Julia Michaels
Sober by Demi Lovato
At My Weakest by James Arthur
I hate you; I love you by Gnash, Olivia O'Brien
Lost Boy by Ruth B.
Let It Go by James Bay
Someone You Loved by Lewis Capaldi
Everything I Wanted by Billie Eilish
When The Parties Over by Billie Eilish
Love Don't Run by Steve Holy
Love In The Dark by Leroy Sanchez
Before You Go by Lewis Capaldi
Love You For A Long Time by Maggie Rogers
Would've Left Me Too by Ryan Griffin
Perfectly Wrong by Shawn Mendes
Warrior by Demi Lovato
Crazy Girl by Eli Young Band
Like I Loved You by Brett Young
Tomorrow by Chris Young

ACKNOWLEDGMENTS

This was one of those books that took all of my attention, heart, and soul to write. While I was writing the harder parts of Tayla's story, I'll be honest; I wanted to stop or to give up. Tayla was a character that was so dear to me, as an author and I was afraid of messing up her story. Because of the amazing, supportive people surrounding me, I was able to push through those worries and make this book what you've read today. First, I need to thank my sister, *Vicky* for being there for me over the past few months. You stuck with me and supported me, as you always do and I love you like crazy. Family has always been so important to me, so I'd also like to thank my parents for believing in my dreams and fostering them as they have. My bestie, *Heather,* you always have my back and when I wanted to give up on this story; you wouldn't let me. *Tracy,* you are so much more to me than just my PA, you stick by my books like they are your own and more than that, you're the best friend I could ask for. Thank you!

I want to extend a BIG thank you to my lovelies.

You girls rock and have so much love for my Alphas and I love y'all for that! Thank you so much, babes.

My betas, *Amy, Sharon, Amanda* and *Mona-* you have helped me hone this story and make it be the almost perfect gem it is. I can't wait for you to read Ben next.

My cover designer, *Mary Ruth.* You are amazing! So, thank you.

Amy, I want to thank you, too. You have helped lift my spirits and share my books when I've been either too distracted or to down on myself self and I'm blessed to have you in my corner.

Harper, thank you for being such a good friend to me while I've fretted over making this story perfect. You're the best!

Lastly, my amazing-as-hell girlfriend- thank you for showing me that love isn't always perfect but it is always, ALWAYS worth fighting for. I love you so much, baby.

If I've forgotten anyone, know that if you've commented, chatted or bought Tayla's book- I love you. Writing what I love and having such support from this community of book lovers continues to surprise me and it's why I'll keep writing, always.

XO Amanda

ABOUT THE AUTHOR

NY Times Bestselling author, Amanda Kaitlyn lives in New England with her girlfriend and her shih Tzu, Mocha. As a girl, she always loved fairy tales but learned the ones she loves are a bit dirtier, now. In her books you'll find raw, real, emotional romance and alpha males that stop at nothing to protect the head-strong women they love. When she isn't writing on her laptop, you can find her playing with her pup or reading on her kindle.

Want to keep up with the latest news & books by Amanda Kaitlyn? Follow her on Social Media and join her readers group for more

CONNECT WITH ME!

Join my Reader's Group @amandakaitlynslovelies
Read on for the first chapter of Ben & Nat's story!

Follow Me
Facebook: @amandakaitlynauthor
Instagram: @amandakaitlyn_author
Twitter: @amandakaitlyn93
Pinterest: @amandakaitlyn
Book+Main Bites: @amandakaitlynauthor

PREVIEW OF REMEMBERING BEN

THE BEAUTIFULLY BROKEN #6

Prologue
Ben

"Maybe I should drive," I muttered as I watched her round the Jeep, tilting her head up to glare daggers my way with narrowed, yet amused eyes.

"Maybe you should shut it, Benjamin Jones."

I laughed at her use of my full name as I got into the car and watched as she checked her mirrors three damn times, adjusting her seat as if it wasn't in the same position it always was.

Jesus. We were most definitely going to be late for Christmas with my family. Few transgressions wouldn't be forgiven by my mother and being late to one of her many family gatherings was one of them. I dropped my head against the headrest with a thud and sent up a prayer that for once in her life, my wife would drive the speed limit.

I loved her, more than anything.

She was my world. But, fuck, she was a terrible driver.

"I'm just saying that we only have twenty minutes to get there."

"It's only a five-minute drive." She said on a sigh, one filled with exasperation for me, one I'd heard so many times before. On a smirk, I reached for her hand across the seat, giving it a playful squeeze.

"Exactly my point, Sunshine." Her blue eyes slanted my way and lifting her hand to my mouth, I kissed her there; knowing she'd melt for me. She always did.

"Fine, you have a point. But I'm driving back." Finally, she conceded.

"Oh, thank God." I sighed dramatically, just for her. Opening the drivers' side door for her, she begrudgingly got out of the car, muttering under her breath that she drove just fine. I just chuckled in her ear, lowering my mouth until I found her cherry red lips, took a long, slow pull of her sweet taste before letting her insistent hands push me away. I'd have her to myself, soon enough, anyway.

"You're making us late, Ben."

"You love it. Now get in." Another eye roll but she complied.

She was a spitfire.

And all fucking mine.

"You ready?" Blowing her long, red hair away from her eyes, she graced me with a smile bright enough to melt the sun. It was one of the many, many reasons I adored her and the reason I called her my sunshine. She lit up my whole damn world.

"As ever."

~

"Do you really have to go, Uncle Ben?"

"Unfortunately, you're mean Auntie says we do." I didn't have to lift my head to see Natalie's eyes narrowing at me as she shrugged on her coat by the door. I had been working late all week on renovations at the recording studio my brothers and I owned and knew the time spent there took away from our sparse alone time at home. I'd promised her we'd leave early from my parent's house tonight, end Christmas Eve right.

Under the sheets.

Fuck.

My cock twitched to life at the thought and bending down in front of my niece, Heather, I ruffled her hair. She was the sweetest little girl I'd ever seen and I made sure to tell her. Not that her older sisters hadn't been, but I was a sucker for this one. She was too cute for her own good and as she looked up at me with that damn puppy dog look on her face, I was sure she knew it, too.

"But I haven't even opened my present yet." Laughing gently, I lifted her off of her feet and carried her toward the front door where my Sunshine waited for me. She just shook her head at me, knowing I'd blame her for us leaving so early. What could I say? I didn't want to let this little angel down.

"We'll be here bright and early for breakfast and presents, Pumpkin."

Her big, green eyes twinkled with excitement and nodding her head, I let her down and watched her scurry off toward the Christmas tree. Its twinkling lights reminded me that we hadn't decorated the one at home. We'd have to rectify that, as soon as I got my grumpy girl home.

"You're such a jerk," Natalie mumbled into my

neck once I pulled her in close, settling her face against my chest while my arms wound around her curvy waist, needing the feel of her before taking the ride home.

Our home.

"You love me, though." Her thin arms wrapped around my neck as soon as the words were out of my mouth and she smiled softly, in the way she often did when she felt thankful for what we had.

We were having a lot of those moments lately. The Holidays brought it on, especially with her fathers passing this past year. I knew she was mourning in her own way, but I also knew she missed him and felt she had to soak up all her time with me; as if she'd lose me, too.

I would never let that happen. She had me, for always.

"Let's go home." I nodded, wrapping one arm around her shoulders and shrugging on my jacket before we headed out into the nippy winter air. Of course, it was Texas; it hadn't snowed. It was just cold.

"You want to drive, honey?"

"No, I promised you could. Just try to get us home by midnight."

"I don't drive that slow!" She rounded on me, those little hands of hers planted firmly on her hips as if that would cause me to change my mind. If anything, it only made me want to tease her more, to see more of her fire and sass.

I grabbed one of her hands over the hood of the car as she opened her door and grinned widely, just to see the soft, beguiling smile she'd give me in return.

"Yes, you do. But I'll keep you." Her free hand

slapped against her chest as she heaved a sigh, like the one I'd given her in the car hours earlier. I just smiled wider at her antics.

"Oh, thank god!" Sass dripped from her teasing voice and I had the urge to bend her over the car, right here in front of the house. Consequences be *damned*.

"Get in the car, Sunshine. Don't make me spank you over the hood. Or would you like that?" I watched as her pale face reddened quickly and she covered her face with her hands, groaning behind them. *My dirty girl.*

"Ben!"

"I know you like it, Nat. Don't be shy."

She glared my way, but she was still blushing.

God, she was beautiful. I couldn't wait to get her home.

"Get us home. I want to fuck you into Christmas, baby."

Her cheeks reddened again but thankfully, she started the damn car.

"I have another test with the doctor tomorrow," Natalie said into the quiet of the car, her eyes planted on the road in front of her, avoiding my surprised stare as the meaning behind her words settled between us.

"What?" I sat up straighter in the seat, suddenly tense all over. I must have heard her wrong, I told myself. We hadn't gone in to see her gynecologist, Dr. Flynn in weeks, hell, it could have longer than that if I was honest with myself.

We were trying for a baby, had been for almost a year now.

A few months back, we both decided to leave it up to fate. It wasn't that we'd changed our minds on wanting to start a family because we wanted it so much.

But enough with in-vitro treatments, fertility meds, special diets.... To watch her get weaker and weaker with each doctor's visit, it was killing me inside. I would have done anything to stop the pain of knowing her body was failing her, in the most important of ways.

I knew how much she wanted to be a mom and would have caught the fucking moon to give her just that. It just didn't seem to be the right time. At least, that was what we had told ourselves.

The treatments the doctor had been giving her were ripping the once strong, beautiful woman I'd married apart and I wouldn't stand for it.

Not now. Not when she'd just lost her father and didn't need the added stress.

And she'd agreed. Yet, somehow she'd gone behind my back and was going back to the fertility center to see Doctor Flynn.

What the fuck?

She was lucky she was driving because if she wasn't I surely would have striped her ass.

"Don't be mad I just—"

"We agreed, Nat. Did we not agree?"

Her eyes- bright with a painful mixture of sadness and hope and brimming with unshed tears- slid over me before returning to the road and I knocked my head against the headrest, ready to blow at the thought of her keeping something like this from me. It wasn't that I wanted to stop her from having a baby or having another envitro treatment if that's what she wanted, I just didn't want her to be hurt anymore.

Jesus. Clenching a rough hand in my hair, I sent up a prayer for strength right then because I didn't know what to do. If my beautiful girl was hiding things from me, *what else didn't I know?*

How had we fallen so far from the open and honest relationship we'd always had?

We didn't do that. We never had secrets. At a time, yes, we had.

Every couple has secrets from one another in the beginning; before you open up and commit. But that wasn't us. We were a team.

We didn't have secrets!

"No, you agreed. I just decided not to push the issue."

"Pull the car over, now. We're talking about this."

"No, you're just going to yell at me." She whisper-spoke and though she was right, I hated the disappointment I heard in her voice. I wished she would have just come to me and talked to me before I lost my shit, but it was too damn late for that. She'd *lied.*

"You're fucking right I will! I told you we were done with all that."

Her heaving breaths and slowly falling tears were the only indicators of her growing emotions but at this point, I didn't care.

"I just—"

"Sunshine!" Panic, white-hot panic speared my chest as I yelled my name for her, my eyes behind her blonde head where the bright lights of a large, loading truck headed straight for us. Somehow she must have missed a light because we were facing head-on traffic and if she didn't get out of the way, it would...I'd reached for the wheel in my haste to get her attention but with the tension of our fight, she pushed back from me; pressing firmer on the gas in the process.

And I realized, among the few seconds before it happened; that I could have avoided it, altogether.

If only I'd driven. If only I had kept a lid on my temper...

But none of it mattered, anymore because it was too late.

The collision happened both in slow motion and in a flash and though I'd tried to shield her the best I could, I couldn't protect my Sunshine from any of it.

I was too fucking late.

Saving Tayla
ISBN: 978-4-86750-022-4
Mass Market

Published by
Next Chapter
1-60-20 Minami-Otsuka
170-0005 Toshima-Ku, Tokyo
+818035793528

3rd June 2021

CPSIA information can be obtained
at www.ICGtesting.com
Printed in the USA
LVHW030424150621
690251LV00017B/1227